6 - 03

Castaways

Castaways

Stories of Survival

Gerald Hausman

Greenwillow Books
An Imprint of HarperCollins*Publishers*

The text of this book is set in Adobe Caslon.

Map copyright © 2003 by Mariah Fox
Book designed by Chad W. Beckerman

Library of Congress Cataloging-in-Publication Data

Hausman, Gerald.
Castaways : stories of survival / by Gerald Hausman
p. cm.
"Greenwillow Books."
ISBN 0-06-008598-3 (trade). ISBN 0-06-008599-1 (lib. bdg.)
1. Castaways—Juvenile literature. 2. Survival after airplane accidents,
shipwrecks, etc.—Juvenile literature. I. Title.
G525 .H324 2003   813'.54—dc21   2002026364

1 2 3 4 5 6 7 8 9 10 First Edition

 Greenwillow Books

For
Jon Huntress

Contents

Introduction

A few years ago, when my wife and I were living in Jamaica, we took a trip up the coast on a whaler. We were between Port Maria and Port Antonio when a violent storm came up suddenly and threatened to swamp us. One of the passengers in our boat had a bottle in his hand, and when a big wave struck him, the bottle turned into shards. We had never seen waves of such force; worse, we'd never been at their mercy.

Fortunately we got out of that in one piece, but it left some questions in our minds: What would we have done if the whaler had overturned in those twelve-foot angry seas?

Could we have swum the three and a half miles to shore?

I'd been trained as a Sea Scout (the nautical branch of the Boy Scouts of America) when I was growing up, and we had been on Jamaica for many years and had experienced all kinds of stormy weather, but the question of survival at sea now began to haunt me, as a man and as a writer. I was a certified scuba diver and knew my capabilities under the sea. But what about on top of it in storm conditions? Could I handle myself in a riptide? In swells more than twelve feet high?

To answer these questions, I began to swim in the open sea. This is not something I encourage for anyone who has not had previous experience as a free diver (diving without a tank) and long-distance swimmer.

As a trained lifeguard I knew how to swim well, but I had never pushed myself to the limit. So I started swimming alone on the edge of a mile-long reef. In the months that followed, I found myself out beyond it, where the depths ranged from fifty-five to three hundred feet, swimming toward an island two-and-a-half miles distant. The round trip from Blue Harbour to Cabarita Island was about five miles total. The current between

Little Bay on the reef side and Cabarita on the other was so strong that no one attempted to swim it alone. This seemed to be the grandest challenge of all, and once I was in good shape, I set my course for Cabarita.

I learned that by alternating swim strokes—sidestroke, backstroke, and breaststroke—I could handle long distances without tiring. However, an active player in my workouts was the constant silent partner called Fear. Sometimes I faced real threats to my safety—currents and barracudas. Worse than these, stinging jellyfish could, and sometimes did, paralyze my shoulders—fortunately just for a short time, during which I usually floated on my back. But I also imagined secret eyes that weren't there, and once, treading water, I fluttered against my own foot and thought momentarily that my fin was a shark.

On one trip I was stalked by a curious or famished barracuda about five feet long. He followed me almost to the beach, his toothy underbite and cold eye always coming closer. (This particular predator, known for its aggression, was finally caught by a fisherman after attacking a swimmer about a year later.)

Another time, during a tropical depression, I was caught

between a forest of staghorn corals and a battery of coral heads, which left me no choice but to dance on the froth when the tide sucked out and to sort of surf when it came back in. That was a touchy situation, but I managed to get to shore with only one gouge on my right ankle.

In a similar predicament, while cruising the coast with mask and fins, I was suddenly sucked into a marine cave. Then I was hurtled through a barnacled tube that spiraled twenty feet or so and let out into a mysteriously quiet azure cove.

Cramping is probably the solitary swimmer's worst enemy. I learned to give myself calf and leg massages in those rough waters where I was a mile or more from shore.

One of the things I did to keep my mind entertained while I swam was to work on stories I was writing. Often the tales had to do with mariners who were shipwrecked, and I was able, while swimming, to visualize these unfortunate people. Sometimes I became them, or they became me. Whichever way it was, I began to understand that survival swimming involves much more than being in good physical shape.

I discovered that it was perhaps more mental than

physical. This explained why characters that I was writing about started to seem more human in my writing. They got tangled up, for instance, in sargassum weed and imagined they were being pulled apart by a giant squid. Friendly porpoises turned into hungry sharks, and even a tiny swallow of salt water turned into a life-snuffing tidal wave.

The mind plays all kinds of games with you when the bottom disappears underneath and there is nothing left but blue, big blue miles of empty sea, where the swimmer feels the myriad eyes of the deep trained on him. Open-sea swimming brings you face-to-face with the most primal fear there is, that of dying. Sometimes I had to fight back the overwhelming fear of drowning, especially when the shore seemed too far away and the harder I swam toward it, the more it appeared to recede. Optical illusions and mind games are rampant in deep-water open-sea swimming.

Well, eventually, after nine years, I had a storehouse of experiences and a lot of words on paper. But I was not writing a book, and my writing, like my swimming, seemed more for exercise after a while than for any specific purpose. The truth was, I wanted to write a sea adventure, but I did not know what to write about. I couldn't tell endless tales about swimming the north coast of Jamaica.

Then, one autumn when I was back in the States, a close friend, Jonathan Huntress, sent me two boxes of archival maritime tales from his father's nautical library. Dr. Keith Huntress, Jon's dad, had been a well-known author and archivist of shipwrecks and disasters. Some of the books had the scent of salt on their yellowed pages. Most were first-person narratives written in the nineteenth century. With the books came a message from Jon: "My father would've liked knowing that these are now in your possession. Maybe you will be inspired to use them in a book of your own."

These old sea stories came at a pivotal and inspirational time for me. In them I found just what I was looking for, stories of common men and women who were forced to deal with uncommon events at sea or, in one instance, in the Everglades, the sea of grass. All were castaways, who had to learn what it meant to survive. They seemed to lose all sense of time and place. They fumbled and foundered on islands and keys, and some were driven to insanity.

Introduction

Interestingly, the tales I read were not unlike those I invented while I was swimming alone. I felt a great bond with historical people, who had been born in strange times and in faraway lands; they were, I thought, just like me. They were swimmers in the sea of life, struggling to stay afloat.

However, the ocean itself is also an important character. Human beings have never been more absorbed with the mysterious waters of the world than at the present time. Stories that reveal the ocean's hidden fathoms draw our immediate interest. Certainly this is explained by the fact that the ocean makes up three-quarters of our earth's surface. And still the sea has not been tamed or much influenced by human technology or our desire to be one with it.

So we are today not unlike the brave mariners of Homer's time in ancient Greece: still wary, still worried about the next big storm. Rogue waves, tsunamis, hurricanes, and all wild-weather phenomena are our common lot. Ships like the *Titanic* are still being built and still being sunk. The ocean, above and below the surface, is an unknown frontier, as unfathomable as what we like to call the vast reaches of outer space. We will probably never conquer it.

In the six stories I have chosen to write for this book, you will find identifiable characters from human history and legend. However, as I swam farther and farther from shore—in swimming and writing—I became the people I wrote about.

I was one with the widowed woman who found peace in petrel feathers; the marooned sailors who discovered brotherhood and charity on a sunstruck sandspit; the man who cruised around the world in a rebuilt boat and fought pirates and ghosts with his wits; the swimmer who could not drown but could easily die on land; the furious soul who succumbed to madness on an island of beasts; and the seeker of solace on the great river of grass.

All these I became in the swimming and the writing. In the end I know there is nothing better in life than to keep the head and the heart up and, when you cannot see the shoreline, always to put one hand, one word, in front of the other.

—Gerald Hausman
Bokeelia, Florida

The Turtle Island of Peter Serrano

*I*n 1540, off the coast of Peru, a violent storm boiled out of the sea and sank the galleon *María d'Or*. The lone survivor, Peter Serrano, was a Spanish traveler who, when cast away into the spindrift, swam like a sea lion to save his life.

The blue dream he found himself in had no beginning and no end. Yet at length the storm clouds lifted. The setting sun washed over the antlers of a vast coral reef, and the sea deposited Peter in a glassy garden of pink anemones. His stay was short.

From there he was siphoned through a green-and-lilac

lake of reef-buttressed shallows until he came, at last, to the shore of a small, flat sandy cay. Dragging himself up on the beach, Peter thanked his Maker for his deliverance. He was on an island; he was alive. Feeling his limbs for broken bones, he reassured himself he was all right. A few scrapes, but that was all. He'd made it. Peter Serrano had survived.

Rising to his feet, he had a look around.

"What a barren little island," he said as he stared into the hard, storm-washed light of the setting South American sun. There was the oyster-colored sand, the spectral blue sea. Beyond the varying blues, lavenders, violets, the meridian of sea and sun vanished, and the sky turned into a hazy, glazy glare. At first glance Peter determined that the little cay was but a league in length and half that much in width, so it was short and narrow and not a place you could get lost in.

He could see there was nothing living on the island but himself. Not a solitary, bony tree or even the skeleton of one. Not a blade of bearded grass. Not even a rock to cast a feeble shadow from the fierce sun. The whole of it, the entire island, was wind-whipped and woebegone sand, empty sand.

The skeins of surf that wound around the protective reef unwound before they hit this secret bight, this storm-safe haven. And yet its very isolation, the thing that preserved it, kept it bone clean and empty of life.

Peter wondered if he was the only man who had ever set foot upon the place. Most likely he was.

That first night Peter lowered his head and wept. "Father," he sobbed, "I don't mean to demean Your saving my life, but I must ask You a question: Have I been spared only to die a slow death?"

There was no answer except for the pounding breakers.

Peter fell asleep with his body curled like a question mark.

Before the sun rose, Peter was awake. He set out to explore his open-air prison cell and to find out if there might be an answer to his prayer. The reef sent up spumes, and from these a mist of vapor curled over the cay. But the sun burned this off, turning the island to a salt white beach. The sand, in fact, was so white it reflected the sun, so that it tortured the bottoms of Peter's feet less than it would've had it been darker. Anyway, when his feet got too hot, he cooled them in the surf.

There must be something to eat, he thought. Some way to shelter my skin from the sun, for already he was beginning to burn. Fortunately he still had a shirt on his back, a pair of pants, and the small knife he always carried with him. These were his only possessions.

The island yielded nothing. The sun beat like a gong. The ocean reared and roared and quieted. Then it repeated the same syllables with the same retractable violence as before. Peter's ears were full of the surf, but his eyes constantly worked in the hope of seeing something. On the eastward end of the island he was rewarded for his vigilance. There were some half-sunken sea rocks on which were encrusted a number of cockles and whelks. With his knife he cut them loose and, having no way to make a fire, ate them raw. They were salty and tough, but he swallowed them gratefully.

That evening before going to sleep on the sand, he looked into the heavens. The stars were foggy and faint and far away. In his home in the mountains of Spain they had seemed so much nearer, more friendly. Here they were pale ghosts of those bolder, closer stars.

As he would at home, Peter said a prayer. "I thank You, Father, for the food You have provided for my sustenance. But I wonder what I will eat on the morrow, and the morrow after that. On the sea rocks there are only so many whelks. I have counted them. No more than twenty are left. What will I do when the mollusks are gone? What am I to drink? My throat is on fire, for I have thirsted greatly, and I have only my own urine. Am I to die of thirst?" However, Peter was so exhausted that he fell asleep soon after this, believing that the Lord was good and kind and that somehow He would see to his salvation.

When he woke, the sun was upon him with a vengeance. Peter looked beyond the soughing of the surf. The horizon was a line as finely drawn as if laid down by a draftsman. Between Peter and the line were gradations of extraordinary aquamarine color—gold, green, violet, and the deepest blue Peter had ever seen. There was, he felt, a ringing emptiness to the blue of the ocean and the bright, fish-scaled light of the moon-driven tide.

He tried to swallow. His throat felt as if it were full of dry cotton. He tried to spit; he could not. He got up and walked. The sun stung his neck and arms and legs.

He was red all over, and his skin was tender.

He walked for a while on the burning beach. With each step he felt his skin tighten, and the little prickles of sand were like fine needles when the wind blew. Some distance off, near the island's northern end, Peter saw a sea turtle. He went over to it and cut the creature's throat with his knife. Then he drank its blood. After this, he butchered some of the turtle's flesh, and he sucked on it until the meat was pulp. Finally, he cut the turtle up into choice fillets and laid them out on some dry seaweed to roast in the sun.

The innards of the turtle contained water, and fat was another bounty. He rubbed the oily fat on his skin, and it soothed the burn from the sun. The sargassum weed pulled straight from the sea was quite edible, too. Peter ate it as often as he felt like swimming out and harvesting it. So altogether he felt much better.

"Father," he said, "I thank You for Your kindness. I feel I could live another day, and the day after that. With Your grace, I might live yet awhile longer. I thank You, Father." In the open air his voice sounded odd to him, almost as if it were someone else's.

Soon after he'd said this prayer, Peter observed the turtle's carapace. Then he picked it up and raised it over his head, and he saw that it was a shield against the sun. For the first time since he'd come to the island, Peter Serrano smiled.

In the days that followed, Peter often found sea turtles. They had huge carapaces as round as shields. From the fresh meat he garnered his food, and from the guts he got water, and from the shells he built himself a suit of armor to ward off the ferocity of the sun. With a shell over his chest, and one over his back, and each suspended by a string of woven turtle skin, he had himself a house. In addition, he used a medium-size shell to make a helmet and dried turtle gut string to secure it under his chin.

"Father," he said, "You see that I am all turtled up now. Every part of me is covered. I am safe from the sun, I am eating, I am drinking what drink I find, and all things considered, I am alive and well, thanks to Your blessings, and may they continue to flow."

Thus did Peter Serrano live and pass his time.

And he ate his daily bread of sun-cured turtle meat.

And he spread his skin with turtle fat. And in the months that came and went, he began to think like a turtle that wants nothing but sees much and lives by its eyes and ears and the beat of its slow heart. On that scant, sun-spattered island, there was little enough to see, but Peter saw it plainly, and saw it well. Moreover, he was rewarded for his visionary patience and his vigilant prayers. These made him feel strong. Still, there was something missing, something that food, water, watchfulness, and prayer would not attend and could not reach. Could it be that he longed for some human company? The thought as such didn't occur to him. But the longing in his belly was there when he went to sleep and often when he looked at the indifferent sea.

The dry season passed, and the wet season started. The sun was less hot, and the winds came crisply, and they brought rain with them. Peter now had a collection of turtle carapaces into which the rains fell. One day he counted a hundred of them gleaming in the sun. The rain had filled them. Peter drank what he needed, covering the rest with other shells, and burying them in the sand.

In this manner, living one day at a time, Peter overcame

the demons of hunger and thirst. And many years passed without his being aware of the passage of time. One morning, when he was at prayer, Peter saw something that curled eerily around the northern lip of his island.

"What can it be?" he asked.

The word came to him slowly. *Smoke*. His curiosity aroused, Peter humped along the beach to find out what was making it. His powers of reason did not immediately admit to the word *man*. He couldn't think that far ahead. He moved clumsily on the sand, somewhere between a crawl and a walk. There was no hurry, and the less he moved in the cruel sun, the better.

When he came to what made the smoke, he crouched in astonishment. An upright man had built a fire and was preparing to cook something on it. The word escaped Peter's lips. "Fire," he said appreciatively. The sound was like steam from the crevice of Peter's mouth.

The stranger looked up. Peter started to drag himself forward. Defensively the man raised a firebrand to protect himself.

"Stand back, creature of the devil," he cried as Peter approached.

Peter lowered his head, his shell hat shadowing his face. The man's fire stick glanced off the turtle helmet. Peter scrunched down and began to mumble a series of incoherent prayers. The stranger, seizing an offensive advantage, beat Peter's head like a gong.

The blows had no effect. Peter crouched lower in the sand.

The stranger struck him all over. Now Peter knew he was in real danger, and he did the first thing that came to mind: He escaped to the sea. The stranger chased him out into the breakers but was then loath to follow. Looking more like a turtle than a man, Peter paddled smoothly over the bone white shallows. Openmouthed, the stranger watched him recede down the cay.

For Peter the rest of the day went by slowly and prayerfully. Boldly he asked the Father, "Why have You given me a cruel soul mate? Someone who wishes to bludgeon me to death? Am I not worthy of this person's company? Is he not worthy of mine? Must we live apart on this tiny mustard seed of sand?"

Saying these words, Peter, perhaps for the first time since he'd been marooned, felt sorry for himself. He began to cry. The tears washed over his cheeks and were lost in his beard. "If these tears were diamonds, that man wouldn't beat me away," Peter said in despair. "If my shell were ornamented with filigrees of gold, he would value me, he would treasure me! Yet as it is, he sees . . . what?" Peter wondered what it was the man saw in him, of him. What was he to the man? A creature perhaps? A thing more turtle than human?

In a flash Peter knew what he'd seen in the stranger's eyes: fear! This man was afraid of him. It would be necessary to approach him differently then. Perhaps he might have to divest himself of his turtle shells. When the sun was almost down, Peter stripped naked. Carrying his armor with him, he walked to where the steady smoke plied the empty sky.

As soon as the stranger saw Peter, he threw no blows. Instead he fled in the opposite direction. "Oh, terrible devil," he cried, "deliver me from your kind!"

Peter put down his armor and started running after the man, yelling at the top of his lungs, "Brother, brother, do not fly from me. For I am as human as you are!"

Still, the stranger fled in horror.

Peter consigned himself to his fate. But that night,

when he prayed, he asked the Father, "Why am I to be thus shunned by my brother? Am I Cain? Is he Abel? Is this Eden?"

Amid his many sighs and lamentations, Peter had a powerful thirst. He got up from the sand, and in the starlight he lowered his face to sip from one of his turtle shells . . . and saw . . . an unholy visage.

Peter howled at the stars. "What am I to do?" he asked the Father.

At the same time, he fingered his face and felt the fur that had grown over it. His beard hung to his navel. Why had he not noticed it before? Peter threw himself on his back and stared up at the quivering constellations in the sky.

He let out a little turtle's sigh of sorrow. "I see now, Father, what You wanted me to witness." And he wept freely again, and the tears watered his chest, which was also a solid mat of tangled hair.

"Oh, how dreadful. I *am* a beast," he whispered in despair.

At dawn, having thought out what he would do to save himself, Peter walked naked down the beach again. He walked to where the smoke rose into the sky in a tall, unbroken pillar of gray.

And before the stranger could run away, Peter presented himself humbly with his palms out, and he begged the stranger, "See me now, my brother, as the Father sees me, a poor, poor, bedraggled thing who was washed up on these shores many long—" There he stopped because he had no idea how long he had been on the island.

The stranger, his mouth open, his eyes staring, did not move.

"I am a man," Peter said softly. "I am not a beast. I am the son of the Father, just as you are. I speak the way you do. My heart beats just as yours does. I pray that you understand my message. Please permit me to be in your company. Fear me not, O Brother, for I mean you no harm."

The stranger, when he heard these words, knew then that Peter—for all his vast array of dark wool—was no emissary of Satan.

The two men came near each other and looked into each other's eyes. Peter wept. The stranger trembled. They embraced. And then the man told Peter that at first, when he laid eyes on him, he thought he was half turtle and half man, but knowing no such creature was in existence, he believed him to be the spawn of the devil. Then, when Peter returned, the stranger saw him in yet another incarnation, more frightful than before.

"Why did I frighten you the second time?" Peter wanted to know.

"The second time you were all wool and hair, and so mightily dense was the tangled growth that I truly imagined you were sent by Satan."

Peter regarded himself. In defense against the sun, he had grown a mantle of spidery hair that covered him from head to toe. His beard hung down like an extra appendage. His chest was hairier than a dog's. His arms were covered in black growth.

"Will I . . . look like . . . you?" the stranger wondered aloud.

Peter shook his head. "I have no true knowledge of when I came to this place, only that the Father cares for my every need, and I have no want."

"That is all well and good for you," said the other. "But I have no desire other than to get off this wretched place. Say, man, what ship were you on when you were cast away?"

"The *María d'Or*," Peter replied. He'd not said the name in so long a time that he scarcely knew how it bubbled to his lips.

The stranger wrinkled his brow. "That ship was lost ages ago," he said. "There were no survivors."

"There was one," Peter answered.

Then the man heaped dried seaweed on his fire, and he said, "Whoever you are, and whoever I am, we shall get off this tongue of sand . . . or my name is not Victor de l'Ambroz."

"I am glad to make your acquaintance, Victor de l'Ambroz," said Peter, his voice quavering. "I am called, or I was called, for I haven't been called anything these many years, Peter Serrano."

His name sounded queer to him. Odd and suspicious, as if he'd made it up.

Now, the time passed more speedily for two people than it had for Peter. Sometimes it went slowly. Other times it crawled. But mostly it moved right along. In any case, it was years before a ship saw the column of seaweed smoke on the little cay and came to rescue them.

But even then it wasn't easily done. The currents of the coastline conspired to hold the ship off. Later, when a dinghy was launched, it, too, had some trouble getting in close. At great length, the two were met by mariners; the rescuers screamed at the sight of Peter and Victor.

Heavily shelled and fabulously haired, the two men were frightful, to be sure. And though they cried out that they were human, their rescuers believed them to be devils. It wasn't until Peter and Victor began singing out the Creed of the Apostles that the mariners realized they might be human.

On further inspection, they found the poor wretches had arms and legs, hands and fingers like their own. Their coverings were the problem. So the castaways took them off and stood nakedly in the sun with their hands pressed together in prayer.

Once on the ship, Peter and Victor were given clothing. But still the sailors didn't trust them. The uniformed men drew a breath when one or both of the castaways came too close. Some of the sailors never approached Peter or Victor but stayed well out of their reach while the ship returned to Europe.

Victor took these rebuffs much harder than Peter. Withdrawing into himself, he died. Some say he died of a broken heart from being rejected by his fellow man. In any case, he passed away silently and swiftly.

But Peter lived to tell his tale, and he went all the way to Germany, where for better or worse, people visited him and paid money to view him. He did not shave his long beard or cut his body's unnaturally thick coat of fur. He presented himself as he was, a castaway. When he spoke to people, he told them that he never wanted to forget his ordeal. He said he was determined to tell each and all his story, so that the world would know that unless we work together, we are destined to lead the loneliest lives imaginable.

Peter Serrano liked to tell people, "Once upon a time I was worth not a farthing, but now I am worth many ducats. Once I was all alone, and now I am amid many. Formerly my shadow was low. Today it is high. But does this make me more, or less, of a man? What is man? Is he merely a creature he himself has constructed? Or is he a timeless being made in the image of the Father?"

His audiences thrilled to hear him ask such blasphemous questions. To them it was clear that he was mad. However, Peter was unconcerned with their judgments upon him. He had not lost the keen eye, the watchful nature, the heartfelt manner that his island had shaped in him. He knew very well what he was, but no one else whom he met in his wide-world travels visiting beggars and kings, pirates and princes had even a shred of what he called common sense. It was this, he thought, that set him apart.

No one knows why he was journeying to Panama when he died. Some believe he was traveling back to the island that bears his name on nautical charts. You can see it there, hanging off the edge of Peru, a little bit of fire-flaked, shell-strewn sand carved by the centuries into the shape of a turtle.

The Beasts of Philip Ashton

*P*hilip Ashton was traveling on the Portuguese schooner *Cadiz*, in June 1752, when a rogue wave rolled her on her beam ends and threatened to sink her. In that one powerful thrust, seawater blasted into the stern ports, filled the hold, and the schooner was swallowing the swells and going down. There was no time to do anything, so the captain ordered everyone into the shrouds and yards.

The heeling wind pummeled the *Cadiz*. The tonnage of wheat, packed too high in the hold, was actually causing the ship to sink, but there wasn't any way to lessen the load. Drafts of seawater were sucked into the ports. The *Cadiz* came ever closer to her watery grave. When the poor ship had dropped to six fathoms, her yardarms stuck onto a reef. With a huge crunch, the ship's descent was abruptly stopped.

Clinging to the canvas sails, Philip and the others watched in horror as the mast cracked and swayed and held—but not for long. Just before it split, Philip jumped into the sea and swam for his life. Rising and falling on thirty-foot swells, he was soon parted from the other men. Alone on a seesawing mountain of moving water, Philip was swept like a bit of balsa from the top of one wave to the bottom of another. Twice he went under and kicked his way to the surface.

The thought of drowning terrified him. Yet the current, it seemed, longed for land, and it carried Philip toward the Triangle Islands, of which there are three, some forty leagues off the coast of Suriname. Once, in wild despair, he thought the sea would overpower him, but then he swam harder. He was determined that he should not drown. There was no death worse, he thought, than going down with a bellyful of salt water.

As luck would have it, Philip made it to the first Triangle Island by sunset. He was painfully sorry to be all by himself, but when he set foot on the beach, he kissed the sand. He was not a religious man generally. However, he was a thankful one when disaster spared his life. He looked around. Whatever island it was, and at that moment he didn't know, it was big. He couldn't see it end to end. Its center seemed to be as dense as the forests back home in England.

That night he stepped up from the beach and found a tree splendidly arrayed with golden fruit. This piece of luck flattered him into thinking that he was twice blessed by Fortune. Thrice blessed, it turned out, for the fruit was delicious. He ate a dozen wild, thick-skinned, glowing oranges. Then, patting his stomach with pleasure, he fell asleep under the tree.

However, that night he dreamed of beasts. Nameless, faceless, they waited in the darkness. "What are you waiting for?" he cried in his sleep. The beasts tried to drag him off with them. Philip clung to the orange tree. He clung to the tree as the beasts pulled at the joints of his legs. He could feel his bones cracking.

When Philip woke, out of breath, it was morning. The dream beasts were gone, but there was a saltwater crocodile near him. Philip took one look at the cold, gold gleam in the dragon's cunning eye. Then he leaped up in a spray of sand, scrambling for safety. The animal didn't give chase. But Philip knew it would be waiting for him when he came back. He'd heard plenty of stories of these loud dragons and of their appetite for human flesh.

There must be a safer place, deeper in the island, he reasoned. But in truth, he was afraid of going any deeper in. He knew nothing of the creatures that lived within the interior of the island. And what of the craven beasts that slunk in and out of his dreams? He could not believe they were just figments of his imagination. He regarded dreams as real. Mariners were always talking of monsters, sea beasts of all sizes and dangerous ape-things that lived on the islands of the tropics.

Thinking these uneasy thoughts, Philip stepped warily into the jungle. The treetops were hung with creepers. There was indeed a dense tangle of timber, and the trees grew inches apart. With some misgiving, Philip entered the grottoes of the ground-draped leaves. Wild birds and grunting feral hogs greeted him as he crashed through their lair. The damp air was heavy with pig musk and bird guano. He longed to be out of there, back on the beach. But there was the sea dragon, the crocodile.

Resting under a plume of fern, Philip saw a pretty yellow-and-brown serpent glide on the dappled leaves. Its head was shaped like a blunt arrow. A little later another serpent, a fat anaconda, went by slowly. The anaconda was longer than he was and thicker than his thigh.

Seeing the cruel serpents, Philip shivered. It came on him again: the ill feeling about the island and his ability to stay alive on it. He left off this gloomy thought, though, when he saw something in the rotten leaf litter at his feet. Philip unearthed a rusted yet usable ax head. "So," he said aloud, "there were people on this place . . . or there still are." He started back to the beach. The rusted ax head gave him renewed confidence. But at the same time, he reasoned that whoever owned the ax might have been killed by one of the many slithering, crawling, hunkering beasts that owned the place.

The crocodile was gone. Philip found a stone and began to sharpen the edge of the ax head. In doing so, he chipped off a little spark that ignited some dry moss. Miracle of miracles, he'd accidentally started a fire! He fed it sticks and it grew, and he kept it burning. His luck didn't end there either. Around noon he saw something brown out on the tidal flats. Ax in hand, he swam out to see what it was.

The thing lay in the shallows. He still couldn't see clearly what it was, so he dived and discovered a giant clam. Another gulp of air, he went under again. This time he saw the clam's mouth was open, and lying on the soft grayish flesh was a magnificent pearl. Once more Philip surfaced and dived. This time he reached into the clam's jaws and plucked out the pearl. His hand was halfway out when the clam closed on his wrist. Although the surface shimmered inches above his brow, Philip couldn't get to it now. The bright, gleaming mirror cruelly beckoned.

Philip jerked madly about before he realized the clam wasn't stationary. He could, after a fashion, lift it up, breathe, and walk with it to the shore. This he did. When the gentle tidewater was tickling his knees, Philip looked off to his left. Something dark and long was coming at him. He saw the great blunt head, and then it struck hard at the ankle and spun him around, knocking him off-balance. It wasn't the crocodile; it was a shovel-nosed shark. The strike felled Philip like a tree. He rolled in the shallows, struggling to get up with the clumsy clamshell. The shark swung around to make its kill.

Philip got to his knees, then to his feet. With another effort he brought the giant clam up to his chest and, at the same time, dug his heels into the sand. The shark came on fast. As it turned its smiling mouth, Philip smashed the clam into its yellow cat's eye. The blow sent the shark rolling and Philip stumbling away. He kicked, floundered, and finally fell top-heavy on the gray, sandy shore. The shark thrashed for some time before it thrust out into deeper water, its dorsal fin canted to one side, its broken eye leaking blood.

When he recovered, Philip inspected the clam. Unfortunately the ax head lay in the water where he'd dropped it when the clam's mouth closed on him. However, Philip's fire was still alight. He blew on it, nursed it with twigs, and got a good blaze going. When the fire was hot enough, Philip put the giant clam on the flames. When he pressed the animal's hinge against the heat, the great mouth quickly gaped open with a sighing sound and revealed a wet bluish mass of pulpy but edible flesh. His hand was free, and he still had the pearl.

Once the clam was well steamed in its shell, Philip tore at the hot, juicy meat. It was good, and he ate until he was full. After this he returned to the orange tree and quenched his thirst with fruit. He was richer for the pearl and wiser as to the shark. Moreover, he'd eaten his fill and had some meat left over. This he wrapped in palm leaves and buried in the moist sand. All he had to do now was retrieve his ax head and things would be well.

That night Philip had more troubled dreams of apish man-things that crept about like cats. Once he imagined one of them was prying his eyes open. But when he blinked, there was nothing there but a bad smell that hung in the air. He checked his trouser pocket for the pearl. The round, silky feeling of this small treasure made him feel secure. He remembered a story he'd learned as a child in England. It was about a boy in biblical times who defeated a dragon with a pearl of wisdom. The lustrous gem spoke to the boy, and its light led him to the east, where he was given a bright robe that he wore to his Father's house high up on a great mountain.

Remembering the ancient story made Philip feel strong. He said to himself, I own the pearl of wisdom; I can defeat dragons. The day beasts and the night beasts be damned, he thought. I have my pearl. But when he fingered its silken surface, he felt again the damp paws of the ape-thing that wanted to steal his eyes.

For breakfast, Philip ate more of the clam meat. He found it distasteful. Already it was turning rotten. So he spit it out and waded into the low tide and retrieved the ax head. On his way back he found turtle eggs that spilled out of the ruffled sand where he scuffed his feet. Still hungry, Philip roasted the leathery eggs in their shells, using a spear of palmetto for a skewer. Another visit to the orange tree wiped away the salty memory of the gamey eggs. Thus he began his morning with something in his stomach.

Days went by in a similar fashion. Then weeks. After which months passed. Philip prospered, in his way. Using his sharpened ax, he carved a cave out of the dunes. He fortified the roof with timber and covered it with dry sea oats and thatch palm. Building a fire in front of the cave, he was safe from both serpents and dragons, and he ate well and slept soundly. With food, shelter, and fire, Philip's life wasn't too bad. There was always the spiritual good that he got from looking at his pearl, too. One gaze into its opaque heart, and he glowed from within and felt himself robed in light like the boy in the parable. The beasts visited him less and less, and only at night or in the very early morning. When they came, he dazzled them with the pearl. Transfixed by the light coming off it, they slowly retreated. The power of the pearl served him well.

Eating shellfish and wild figs and drinking sea grape tea steeped in a calabash with rainwater gave Philip's life a certain predictable order. One morning, when he'd been on the island close to a year, he saw a small canoe coming toward him from the calm, windless sea. Silhouetted against the white sky was the dark shadow of a man. His paddle raised, dipped, and dropped. The canoe came closer.

Philip didn't know what to think. He was full of vague, uneasy suspicions. He tried to banish them by rolling the pearl in his pocket-hidden palm. The light rose and warmed his chest; he felt better. He waited. The canoeist was an old man. The silence between them was broken only by the soft lisp of the surf and the far-off wail of seabirds.

Finally, the old man asked, "Friend?"

Philip replied, "Friend."

The old man guided the canoe and came ashore. He and Philip pulled the canoe up onto the beach. The old man offered Philip his hand, and they clasped. Then they nodded formally. Philip felt sheepish. He was not used to people, and evidently the old man felt the same way. They were mutually resistant to each other. But gradually the suspicion left their eyes. After all, they were just two human beings on an island. They did not have to be suspicious of each other. They could be friends. Why not? What was preventing it?

"Where are you come from?" Philip asked.

The old man grinned, showing that he had good teeth. "I am from Spanish Cay, southward of here."

He stood narrow-shouldered, snowy-haired. His skin was light brown, not dark. His palms were placed on the top of his paddle, which was resting, blade end, in the sand. The seabirds mewed in the bay, looking for something to eat.

"How long have you been in the islands?" Philip asked.

"I was twenty-two years among the Spanish. My original home was north Britain, but I came here when I was in my middle age. It was all right living with the Spanish, but they came last night and said they would burn me out if I didn't leave. It seems they are hard at war with my country, or what used to be my country, for I have no country to call my own . . . anymore." The old man smiled. His blue eyes twinkled. "But what of you? How long have you been here?"

"Some time, I suppose."

"Is it good?"

"Not bad."

The old man scratched his head. "Are you . . . English?"

Philip said he was.

"May I join you then? My name is William."

"Mine is Philip, and I shouldn't mind," Philip said. "You know, someone to talk to." He felt the pearl in his pocket.

The old man peered at him. "Is there anyone else here?"

"Well," Philip answered, "to be truthful, there are others."

The old man gave him a startled look. "Others?"

"Beasts," said Philip. He stroked the pearl.

The old man eyed the jungle, as if he felt them lurking. "What kinds of beasts?"

Philip smiled slyly. "Day beasts and night beasts."

"You mean the usual. Crocodiles. Hogs. Lizards. Snakes."

"And more," Philip replied.

"More?"

"Yes, the creatures of darkness are not always visible. Nor do they present themselves in the flesh."

The old man said with resolve, "For beasts, I have this!" He reached into the load of goods in his canoe and held up his musket.

Philip smiled weakly. "That won't ward off the beasts on this island." Then he added, "I have a pearl."

The old man glanced into Philip's eyes. What he saw there gave him a little chill. However, he shrugged it off. The fellow's been alone too long, he thought.

For the next hour or so they unloaded William's canoe. There were five pounds of salt pork, a knife, a bottle of gunpowder, tobacco, tongs, flint, some canvas, and other provisions. All this they stacked to one side of Philip's cave house.

William liked the cave, but he thought it was precious little considering what Philip might have accomplished.

"Those beasts of yours must keep you on the run. I tell you, I had a regular little fort built over at my island."

Philip squeezed the pearl.

The old man cocked his eye at him. "Don't worry, I'll build a better house for us here. Wait and see. I'm very good with my hands." Then he fell to organizing his things.

Philip watched in silence, and he rubbed his thumb on the pearl concealed in his pocket. The old man doesn't believe in the beasts, he thought, but he'll soon learn.

By noon, working all by himself, William had strung out his canvas. He had made a large, sun-shaded enclosure supported by tall stakes. Underneath the canvas, the cool shade was inviting, and the breeze from the sea passed through pleasantly.

That night William broiled a delicious meal of salt pork. To brighten the cave, he lit some fragrant-smelling pitch pine. Philip was surprised. He didn't know the branches had any sap in them. But then he'd never really concerned himself with the trees that grew on the island. The orange tree was his favorite, but he'd long ago picked it clean, and it hadn't produced a new crop yet.

"Have you eaten meat in a while?" William asked, wiping the grease from his lips.

"You mean, beast?"

William seemed annoyed. "I mean, wild hog."

"No," Philip answered.

They chewed in silence. The pork was too salty, Philip thought. Afterward his stomach troubled him. He wasn't used to the fat or the salt. He held his belly all night, and he had a terrible dream.

An ape-thing came into the cave and carried him off into the jungle. It smelled of sulfur, its matted coat was wretched, and its eyes were deep-set fire coals. Philip had nothing to protect himself with except the pearl. When the beast threw him on the ground and prepared to tear his heart out, Philip reached into his pocket and produced the glorious little orb, the pearl. The ape snarled, drew back its big-browed, shaggy head. The pearl cast off many colors that dazzled the beast's eye. It shrank away from Philip. Suddenly William appeared from within the creature. He walked out of the beast's awful hide and said, "Give me the pearl!" And Philip answered, "I will never give it you." They wrestled in the wet leaves and rolled all about, and William growled and showed his fangs. Philip woke, his heart thumping. He looked over at William, who was sound asleep. The old man was no longer a friend.

After William got up, he told Philip he was going to shoot a deer on the Triangle Island that was to the east of them.

"Do you want to come with me?"

Philip shook his head. "Someone ought to stay here," he said.

"Suit yourself."

Carrying his musket, some powder, and a leather bag of lead, William got into his canoe and waved. "Be back shortly," he said, and shoved off.

Philip watched intently as the old man paddled into the distance and was gone around the corner of the island.

That afternoon the sky clouded up, and the water got choppy. Philip looked toward the place where William had gone. The dark sky looked ominous over there. Maybe William was caught in the rain. In a storm. Drowning at sea. Strange, he thought. It doesn't bother me, his being gone. To Philip, the old man was like the last person on earth, and yet he didn't care what became of him. He cared only about what became of himself . . . and the pearl. The rain fell in sheets. Philip watched it from the dark sanctuary of his cave.

Time went by; William didn't return.

In a dark mood, Philip decided the old fellow was dead. Then, one morning, William's canoe drifted into the mangroves. The sight of it gave Philip a queasy feeling. He looked inside. Empty.

That afternoon a Spanish brig cruised into the bay and routed Philip out of a good nap by firing at him.

The long guns flashed from the mastheads. The shots kicked up sand on the beach. Philip was stung as one of the lead balls grazed his right arm. The bullets bit into the sand; Philip ran for safe cover. He got to the mangroves where he'd tethered the old man's canoe. The lead whined in the wet green glades of the sunless lagoon. Bullets thunked into the roots and made the black crabs scuttle backward, pincers upraised.

Philip got into the canoe and paddled far into the mangrove swamp. The tree roots resembled spiders and serpents, and the smell was oppressive, clammy, and stale. Yet in a short while he'd crossed the island's steaming interior, and the sharpshooters had stopped plinking. He was out on the other side of the cay, where the wind froze the sweat on his skin. A flock of nervous snowy egrets pummeled their wings to get in the clear. He paddled on the dappled sea. His canoe cast the only shadow on the crystal bay.

On this leeward side of the Triangle, the sand was cinnamon. The air was dry. In the tucked-up rocks the spiny trunk of a cactus reached, spindly-armed, into the light. The wind came hard from the west and blew Philip in the same direction William had gone. The Spaniards showed no interest in him, if in fact they saw him slipping away into the green-blue glare.

Philip got to the second Triangle before the sun was high in the sky. Straight off, he found the old man's gear. There, lying in the shade of a coconut tree, William's small oak cask of water. Philip drank from it thirstily. Nearby he turned up William's rusted musket and his lead and powder. All these were lying under the shade of a bloodroot tree, but there was no other sign of the old man.

The heart of the tree had been burned out by a lightning strike. It was almost the same size as his cave. Philip was pleased. He moved into this cavity of darkness, as if he had been born there. But from that day forward life was very different. This Triangle smelled sulfurous and sick. The plants that grew were stunted and pale. Steam issued from holes in the earth. Scorpions came out of cracks, and mosquitoes sang without cessation, day and night. The tree frogs were so loud, Philip's eardrums buzzed. Worst of all, this Triangle had a variety of beasts that were more wicked than those on his old island.

One night, as he slept with the old man's rusty gun pressed close to his chest, one of the beasts snorted near the tree cave. It sounded as large as a man. The beast's breath was sulfury and foul. Philip lay low, rubbing his pearl between his thumb and forefinger. He squeezed it hard, in the hope that the beast would go away.

After a long wait Philip got up and looked into the swollen night. The beast spun on cloven feet; its pronged tail struck Philip a stinging blow on the chin. He fell backward. The beast growled, green eyes aglow. Philip lay on his back, stunned. His pearl had failed him. He told himself, It's the same beast that killed the old man. Then he reasoned, It *is* the old man. Once the pearl had failed him, Philip didn't know what to do.

During the day the sand fleas chewed his flesh. The flies lay in thick clouds about his face, and sometimes he breathed them into his lungs. He watched a green lizard on a throne of leaf. Wearing a frayed collar of skin that it was shedding, the lizard stood stock-still. This gave Philip an idea: He stripped naked. Then he rubbed black mangrove mud all over his body and face. It was like the lizard's skin, and he could shed it if he wanted to. After this he had no need of clothing. Nor did the fleas and the flies ruin his days and nights.

Philip drained the water cask. The rusty gun wasn't good for anything but a battering ram. The flint in the hammer, however, was excellent for starting fires. But the wood of this Triangle wouldn't burn. The beasts slept underground during the day; every night they emerged to devil him. Other things happened, too. When Philip walked to the beach one day, he saw an English cottage with a thatch roof. Strange that he'd not seen it before because it was but a quarter league from his tree cave.

The cottage was painted white; the doorway was

open. Philip's heart jumped when he laid eyes on it, for he knew it would be well stocked with food and water. He walked to it with the greatest purpose. He needed to appear presentable even though his skin was black with caked mud. Philip knew he didn't look English anymore, but he knew how to converse, if he had to, and even though it was useless against the beasts, he still had his pearl in a pouch around his neck. The cottage turned out to be a big rock covered with white bird guano. The top had a growth of grass. The doorway was made by another boulder that leaned against it.

Philip looked into the interior of the boulders. Inside there was a stone ledge with a natural catchment of rainwater. Philip lapped the water until his tongue was raw from the rough rock.

That night he was awakened by a roar. Outside his tree cave there was a hellish tumult. Two ape-beasts were fighting. Philip knew that if they saw him, he'd be torn to shreds. He remained still. The growling and gnashing went on and on. He closed his eyes, drifted off. Then something bit him on the neck. He felt the pinprick of needle-sharp teeth. He struck his neck with his palm and flung a giant beetle off him. The spurs and claws of the beetle had torn his flesh.

In another moment he heard the beasts again. This time there weren't two, just one. The solitary beast shoved its rude head into the tree cave. Philip smelled the stink of crushed beetles. The beast said, "Murther." Then it retracted its shaggy head and clumped away into the palmettos.

Philip wondered if he'd heard it right. Was it *mother* or *murther*? He couldn't be sure. Was it *murder*? He'd no way of knowing. The word troubled him terribly.

In the light of dawn Philip still didn't feel safe. Walking toward the sea, he was fearful of being lost. The old familiar trail was suddenly uncertain. He wavered. Wondered what to do. Then he saw tracks. Odd, sand-dented, dimpled footprints. He followed them. It was a sea turtle. He drew William's knife and butchered the animal. He drank from the turtle's water bladder. It was a female, and there were abundant eggs. Once cracked, they slipped thickly down his throat.

"Murther," he mumbled, "I've murthered a mother."

He said this many times as he wiped the greenish yolk from his chin.

At dusk, feeling full-bellied at last, Philip looked out to sea. A cathedral covered with green moss had risen out of the waves. There was a singing of choirs. The setting sun ignited the stained-glass windows and set them aflame. The sun disappeared into the sea. The cathedral slowly sank beneath the waves into the lavender gloom of evening.

Philip felt wet tears cross his cheeks. "In another moment I'd have walked through the door of that church," he mumbled. He polished his pearl furiously.

That night there were no beasts. The tree frogs were quiet. A moist and palpable silence prevailed. The tree caught some wind toward dawn and made the sound of harpsichords. The leaves parted, and tiny points of stars tickled Philip's mud-cracked face. He chuckled and felt happy for the first time since he'd been shipwrecked. He was so happy. He felt stronger and stronger. He squeezed his pearl. It made his hand, his arm tingle. His body glowed, and the robe of glory radiated the light of the Father's kingdom. The beasts couldn't come near him now. They wouldn't dare.

The next day a passage of birds going south blotted out the sun. It rained hard enough to fill the cask. The refreshing rainwater made Philip feel wonderful.

That night, with water on his side, and his belly full of a dozen more sea turtle eggs, Philip fell into a deep sleep. He dreamed he was swimming to another island. He could see it in front of his eyes. When he got to it, he found brown-skinned, gracious women. The men were out fishing. "What do you call yourselves?" Philip asked. "We've no need of names," the women answered as they fed him spoon after spoon of milk and honey.

He awoke in the hot, wet dawn with a violent stomach-ache. The beautiful dream vanished with the pain in his belly. When he went to relieve himself, a crouching beast followed him. Philip cringed. Yet there was nothing he could do; he was too weak to fight. The beast touched him on the cheek with its cold nose as he got rid of his sickness.

"Don't kill me while I'm so weak," he begged. "My flesh won't taste good. Wait till I've recovered; then eat me."

Philip felt a claw run down his spine. The beast spoke

to him. "Phill-iipp." The voice was low and soft. Its breath smelled of crushed grass and spoiled fruit. He felt some saliva from the beast's mouth water his back. Then he passed out.

When he awoke, he was lying in a hammock. A family of Caribs was caring for him. They fed him herbs, and they gave him a broth of pigeons. They spooned coconut jelly into his mouth. Whenever his lips trembled, an elderly woman with a kindly face gave him a spoonful of sweet nectar. She rubbed his raw skin with the healing oil of the red-shelled crab. He tried to give her his pearl, but she showed him a bag of them that the children played with.

In time Philip was able to eat bananas, figs, yams, fowls, fish, and fruits. After much time he was able to walk and work and help his Indian friends as they fashioned their fishhooks from barracuda bones and carved their dugout boats from burned-out trees.

An immeasurable amount of time went by. Philip lived among the Caribs as one of them. One day some Englishmen came to the island, which was the third Triangle. They discovered Philip living with the

Caribs, and they asked him if he wanted to go with them to the island of Barbados. At first he didn't want to go, but after a while he changed his mind.

"I love them more than I love myself," he said. "Yes, I will love the Caribs as long as I live. . . . I would shed my blood for them anytime they asked."

"Then why do you wish to leave?" one of the Englishmen asked. He had a pointy beard, and he wore a vest of iron.

"I should like to try a drink of hot milk and rum," Philip replied.

The men stared at him. The one with the pointy beard smiled.

"I should like to see more people of my own kind," Philip went on, his eyes shining. "I should like to wear clothes to see what they feel like. And then, after behaving like an English, I shall return here and live the rest of my life among my people."

"*Your* people?" questioned the bearded man.

"These are *savages*," said another.

"I mean to say—" Philip began to answer, but the bearded one cut him off.

"They're cannibals."

"There *are* beasts that live on these islands," Philip replied. "I've run up against them. But these dear, sweet Caribs are not like that. They're not beasts."

The curious Englishmen glanced from one face to another. They cast a doubtful look at Philip. He did not look crazy to them; in fact, he seemed quite sane.

"They eat one another whenever they like," the bearded man said. "Isn't that true?"

Philip shook his head. "No," he said, "that is something we do ourselves . . . here."

He tapped his forefinger over his heart.

The Widow Carey's Chickens

Thirty miles west of Land's End, England, on the coast of Cornwall, there are a group of islands called the Scilly Isles. Their broken cliffs rise out of the Atlantic, and being in the direct track of vessels bound for the English Channel, they were historically the scene of some disastrous shipwrecks.

Six of the islands are of considerable size, and one of them, lying on the southwestern side of the cluster, is called Bryher. This is a bare but rugged island whose hills are thickly jowled and whose toothy coast meets the sea in spumes of feathered spray.

It was off the loud and violent shore of Bryher one October in 1743 that the *James Moffett* went aground. A hurricane from the southwest drove the ship against the dark reef of rocks. She was loaded to the gunnels with goods, and what passengers there were swiftly drowned.

All, that is, but one.

When the ship foundered, the islanders of Bryher began pouring out of their cottages to lend a hand. They gathered at the pounding shoreline by lantern light. There was nothing to be done except watch the white combers break on the black shelf of rocks. With each heaving billow that blew in, there came ashore pieces of the *Moffett*: washed-up deck chairs, boxes, bales, and endless barrels of assorted cargo.

In the sea wash, too, came the broken bodies of human beings. One after another. The faces of the forlorn, waxen, white, and dead. Some clutched drowned children. Others—open-eyed and openmouthed—seemed about to say something. But their lips were frozen, and their tongues still.

Through the weary night and into the dreary morning

the salvagers thronged on the Bryher coast, working in the shadows of their yellow whale oil lamps. When daylight arrived, they saw a portion of the ship's hull just a few cables' length from where they stood.

There was the *James Moffett*, her spars naked to the winds. Her hull a wreck. Her masts as skeletal as winter trees. By day's end the sea had battered the *Moffett* down all the way to her keel. What remained on the black-rocked reef was the faintest shape of a ship, just a little more than a child's sketch.

How many passengers were on the *Moffett* when she went aground, the islanders couldn't say. The bodies kept showing up on the beach.

And then, miracle of miracles, one proved to be alive.

It was a woman in her mid-twenties. She was pretty as a cameo and wet as a rat. The Bryherians carried her to the Inn of the Fishers, which was built in a safe cove close to the shoreline. She was quickly given dry clothes and a warm woolen blanket by some of the fishermen's wives.

For several hours she remained quiet and shaken. Yet after some hot soup and brandy, she decided to tell her tale. Her toneless voice described the deaths of her husband and baby.

"I am the widow Carey," she said. The woman peered at the wondering faces of the people gathered at the inn. "My husband and child were with me on the *James Moffett* bound for Philadelphia from Bristol when we crashed into those awful rocks. That is what has made me a widow, a childless widow."

Her clear oval face was pale and drawn. Her little voice was hard to hear over the roar of the breakers that gnawed at the stormy coastline. "Am I the only one who has survived?"

One of the fishermen spoke up. "How many were on your ship's register, do you know?"

"One hundred or more," she said softly.

The fisherman said, "We found as many bodies as rocks out there, and you're the only one with a living breath."

The widow's eyes were cast toward the sea. Through a window she stared at the reefed sea crags and the outline of the desolated ship.

In the silence of the inn there echoed the grinding sea

and crackling fire. No one said a word. Presently the widow Carey was offered a cup of tea. She accepted it absently. Her eyes roved the room but always returned to the window with the view of the *James Moffett*.

The fishermen and their wives shared glances. They sipped their mugs of tea. No one spoke. Speech is a foolish thing when you have lost everything.

Finally, the innkeeper's wife came forward. She had a voice that could soothe a lifeless stone. She said, "When, dear lady, your physical strength has in some measure been restored by rest, we shall be glad to take you to St. Mary's, and thence to Bristol, and then—"

The widow Carey looked alarmed.

"Oh, no!" she exclaimed. "I could never—" She broke off and stared out the window at the black rocks. "Here I must stay," she said in a still, small voice.

"But you must go home, dear. I mean, one day you must go back to Bristol, or Philadelphia, or wherever your home might be." These were the gentle words of Georgie Barkham, the innkeeper's wife. "Don't worry," Georgie whispered. "The time will come when you'll want to leave."

"I won't ever leave," the widow Carey said. Her eyes stayed on the line of rocks that had broken the *Moffett* into spars fingered by the crests of foam. She asked in a chilly voice, "Do any of you think you could tear me from the place where my husband and child perished?"

The women of Bryher exchanged worried glances. The men drank their tea in silence.

The widow asked, "Who among you knows how my husband in his last hour lashed me to the plank of wood that saved my life? Who here can say how he placed me there with our baby, while he waved me away? Who among you knows how my firstborn, my only born, was torn from my hands by the sea before we ever reached this shore?"

The widow's eyes flashed. The wind sang in the flue, and the fire leaped in the hearth, and somewhere in the darkness a dog howled mournfully.

Now the widow's fluid voice had the sound of a chant. "I pray that you may have pity on my little one's soul, and my brave husband's, and those others who went down on the *Moffett*. I pray you have pity on me, too, though I have been blessed—or cursed, I know not which—to live. In any case, I will remain here for the rest of my days. I won't eat the bread of idleness. I shall assist you in your needs. I shall nurse you in sickness, and I shall sit with you in suffering, as you stand with me now. But you mustn't ever ask me to leave your island."

There was no answer to this startling speech. The fishermen and their wives patted the woman on the shoulder, and one by one, they took leave of her.

The people of Bryher had seen victims of tragedy all their lives. They knew that the misfortune of the widow Carey had affected her reason. They were sure that one day she would come to her senses.

After Georgie put the widow to bed, she told her husband, "One day the poor, distracted darling will beg to leave the barren Isles of Scilly. In the meantime we'll see to her welfare. We'll be pleased to have her among us."

So a pact was passed among the villagers. They were to be the widow Carey's guardians. Until such time.

No one could have guessed how long a time that would be.

Where the widow Carey came to live is as much part of her life as anything else. On a little promontory on the southwestern part of Bryher there was an ancient ruin. Built of stone hundreds of years earlier, this place was shaped like a tower over the sea. Some said it had been crafted by Druid priests.

The tower commanded the only perfect view of the sea crags where the *James Moffett* had met her end. Not surprisingly, this was exactly where the widow Carey decided to live.

At first, Georgie and others brought her food. They sought her welfare. But in time she took better care of them than they of her. She tended the sick and was adept at healing them. She was especially good with children, all of whom loved her. As it turned out, she conversed only with the children of the village. To them she sang little songs in a clear soprano voice that delighted all who heard it. Grown-ups could never get the widow to sing for them; she said she didn't know how. But for the children she was the pied piper of song.

Wherever there was suffering, the widow Carey came and helped. Wherever there was sickness or strife, she appeared. Whenever she departed, those who were in her care had been restored. Yet she rarely ever spoke to those she cared for. She would not take money for her services, but she gladly accepted food and clothing.

Time washed over the headland hill where the widow Carey lived in her stone tower. Fishermen would often see her standing on the top of the battlement. One morning, as three friends were heading to the sea the widow stood out like a statue against the rising sun. "She's a faithful landmark atop that pile of rocks," said one of the fishermen.

A second remarked, "You can set your timepiece by that woman."

The third pointed out, "Some say you can see the headland better when she's standing upright on it. Lord knows, she's like a little lighthouse unto herself."

The years passed, and one generation went away and another was born. In time the widow Carey lived beyond the lives of all who had first met her on that tragic day. Before Georgie Barkham died, she was the only one left who had heard the widow Carey begging to stay on Bryher for the rest of her days. Those days, it seemed, were endless for the widow. But not for everyone else.

The widow Carey, in the passage of time, became a kind of living legend. When people were ill, they saw her at a window. Her pale, thin face; her dark black shawl. Phantom-like, she appeared. But she no longer entered homes to perform her miraculous healings. Her presence was merely felt and only fleetingly seen. Sometimes she appeared to sick people in dreams; after seeing her, they got well.

"How is that?" asked a visitor one cold April morning as he sat before the crackling fire at the Inn of the Fishers.

"Well, sir," Georgie's daughter Susan said sweetly, "she came here more than sixty years ago, as my mother told me. It was before I was born. It happened on the night of the *James Moffett*."

"James Moffett . . . who's he?" the stranger asked, taking a gulp of grog.

"She was a great four-masted ship," said Susan, wiping the bar clean with a calico cloth. "A ship like all ships, though, that find the reef of a stormy night. Well, she was on that ship, the widow was; she was the lone survivor."

The visitor grumbled. "Is that what the legend's all about?"

"Well, anyone else would've left us by now, but not her. Not our widow Carey. She's as much a part of us as we are of her."

"And as little a part, too," put in a fisherman, who clinked tankards with another.

"Yes. She has her ways," said Susan.

"What do you mean by that?" asked the visitor.

"She doesn't talk anymore. Nor does she show up— unless we're sick. Mostly we see her at the window."

"Doesn't anyone go up to that stone house of hers?"

"No one goes up there, except the children."

"Why are you so curious?" asked one of the fishermen at the bar.

"It's my business to be. I'm a journalist."

The fisherman was puzzled.

"I write newspaper articles," explained the visitor. "Let me introduce myself. My name is Keziah Coffin, and by the way, your saint of the sea cliff will make quite a story."

"I wouldn't write about her if I were you," said Susan.

"We'll see," said Keziah Coffin.

Early the next morning Mr. Coffin hiked out to the headland, notebook in hand. He went toward the south and a little to the west, and he found the widow Carey's tower quite easily. She was there, too. In the light of the new-risen sun she was sitting by herself on a flat gray rock. It was really a bench built by those ancient men the Druids. The writer had never seen a more desolate spot. Or a stranger, more lonely figure than the widow Carey. She looked like the last woman on earth.

Slowly he walked to the top of the hill. The wind was blowing hard. At first he tried to make small talk, but his words were lost in the wind. The widow Carey looked blankly ahead, staring into the foamy fingers that grabbed at the rocks. Her long dark veil blew behind her, and she didn't seem aware that anyone else was there.

Keziah Coffin tried to get the widow to speak with him—but to no avail. At last, after staring out to sea for a long time, she got up abruptly and left him. The door of the tower closed with a bang. The writer shook his head. He had questions but no answers. In the end he stumbled back to the inn, more intrigued than ever. In fact, Mr. Coffin wanted to write this story so badly, he could see the words forming in the air in front of his face. But he wouldn't write a word without more facts.

"You're no different from anyone else, I don't suppose," said Susan, who served him hot tea with a biscuit and a salted pilchard. "I don't know how often we've seen her up at that tower. When the fishermen leave at dawn, she's always there. When they come home and the sun's on their shoulder, she's *still* there. Her flag is that dark veil she wears over her face, and it's always blowing in the wind. Did you see it?"

"I stood beside her for the better part of an hour. She was all wrapped up, as you say. Never noticed me. Finally, she got up, went inside her tower."

Keziah Coffin munched down his biscuit. Then, wiping his pink lips, he asked, "Is there anything else about the widow that I might know? I'm itching to write her up. Just itching."

Susan served him a second biscuit. "What do you mean?"

"I need something," he said, "that I could use to build a story on. You know, something that rounds out her character a little. I have to confess, your lady of the tower has me stumped. What's her reason for being so alone up there, all by herself?"

"Maybe that's best left alone, like her."

Keziah Coffin drank his tea and smacked his lips noisily.

Susan refilled his cup.

"Well," Keziah Coffin prompted, "maybe you know . . . some little piece of information that I could—"

"You could start with this," said a little girl, who seemed to appear out of nowhere.

"Who are you?" said the writer.

"I'm her daughter. My name is Georgie," answered the dark-eyed, dark-haired child. "I know the widow better'n anybody. She's my . . . friend. All the children like her."

"Well, come over here and let me have a better look at you."

Georgie came from around the bar, where she'd been helping her mother.

"Don't you go telling him anything outrageous, my sweet," Susan said. "Stick to the facts, if you tell him anything."

"I don't see the harm in talking about the . . . *chickens*," said the child.

Keziah Coffin grinned. "Now we're getting somewhere. What chickens?"

The little girl's face lit up. "They're the lost souls she watches over."

"Lost souls. I see."

"From the people who died on the *James Moffett*."

"I see," said Keziah Coffin. He had his notebook open, and he was writing in it rapidly. "You said they are chickens?"

Georgie's eyes danced. "They're *petrels*. But she's got them so tame everyone on the island calls them chickens."

Keziah Coffin rubbed his brow. It was clear he didn't know what petrels were.

"Seabirds," she told him. "The widow keeps them in her tower at night. She lets them out before sun up. You can see them then."

"And you say they're the souls of the people who died aboard the *James Moffett*?"

Georgie picked up his biscuit plate and his empty mug.

"Don't take that away," he said. "I'll have another of . . .

everything." He patted his big stomach. The little girl laughed and went to get him some more.

When Georgie returned with a second helping, Keziah Coffin asked, "What other wrecks have been on that reef?"

Susan answered this time. "None. Not since the widow Carey came here."

Keziah Coffin jiggled his teacup and studied the flurry of tea leaves swirling in the white of the bottom. "Now that," he said, "is the work of an angel. If, of course, it's true." He shook his head and smacked his lips. "Trouble is, I have a hard time believing any of this."

Georgie's eyes widened. "I can show you her chickens," she said. She traced her finger across the window that looked out on the reef and made two wings in the breath of moisture on the glass.

"How?"

"You've got to get up before the sun."

"All right."

Georgie skipped off. "See you tomorrow, mister."

Next day, well before first light, Keziah Coffin and Georgie, the innkeeper's daughter, went to see the widow Carey. The heavyset man carried a lantern. The girl scrambled ahead of him.

They found the widow Carey sitting on the bench, staring at the ocean. The door of the tower was open. As the sun came out of the sea, a storm of dark-winged petrels fluttered out of the doorway. They settled all over the widow, who never stirred. They dropped like leaves all over her head, her shoulders; every part of her was painted in feathers. And the sounds they made: what weird pipings. What strange singings.

Finally, the widow stood up slowly, and the birds departed. They swung out in an arc around the tower, which they circled three times. Then they descended and followed her inside.

That evening at the inn Keziah Coffin sat before the fire, notebook in hand. He wasn't writing. He stared into the flames. But instead of seeing the darting orange lights of the fire, he saw wings, ashen wings flickering before his eyes.

The next morning before first light Keziah Coffin awoke with a purpose. Once again he headed southwest along the path that wound up toward the widow

Carey's tower. She was there, as usual. Straight and tall, on her bench. He approached as the sun rose. He waited. The petrels didn't come. The door to the tower was closed.

He and the widow looked out at the salmon-colored sky.

Neither one of them moved.

Suddenly a gust swept up from the coast, and the widow folded sideways. Keziah Coffin moved quickly and caught her in his arms. At the same time, the petrels made a gentle thunder as they floated out of the open window casements of the tower. But this time they did not settle on the widow; instead they climbed into the sky.

Keziah Coffin noticed that the widow's eyes were shut. A small smile was on her lips. Her body was hard as wood. Around and around the little storm of petrels whirled overhead. They circled the widow Carey three times, and then they flew low over the breakers and lower still to the reeflike rocks. Then they went out to sea, their high, piercing sea cries keening on the wind, until all Keziah Coffin could see of them was a swirl of specks on the white gold of the sky.

There was nothing to do but tell the villagers what had happened. For some reason, he didn't feel it was his right to disturb the widow's final resting place. On the way back down the hill he met Georgie, who looked up questioningly into his eyes.

"Is she gone?"

He nodded. "They took her away with them."

For a little while they walked in silence.

Then Georgie said, "The chickens never go out to sea. They never do that; they never fly away."

"Well," he said, "since they did, then I suppose the *James Moffett* is finally put to rest."

"Is she all right?"

"You mean the widow Carey?"

Georgie nodded.

"I don't think she's ever been better."

Walking back to the inn, Georgie said, "I'm going to miss her and her chickens."

"I didn't know her and I miss her," Keziah Coffin said.

Today the old rough stone battlement still graces the headland hill of Bryher, and some say there is a time of day when the air stirs and is charged with the gentle thunder of wings. Even now, it is considered a mortal sin to harm a petrel, and when the petrels come to Bryher, some people still call them the widow Carey's chickens.

The Man Who Would
Not Go Bottom

*H*enri Roi was his name.

They called him the man who wouldn't drown. In the late 1940s on the island of Bequia in the Grenadines, everyone knew him, as they know him today, though now he is a very old man. There is something of the immortal in this simple fellow, this swimmer against the odds, against fate, against the death-tolling sea.

Henri cheated death, people say. Not once but a thousand times. And they recite the occasions, now famous, of his evasion of the Reaper.

Why should such a man live when others died? Well, if what they say in Bequia is true, Henri Roi was born with a caul over his eyes. That is, he came out of the womb into the light of day with a thin membrane of skin that shadowed his face. The midwife had to tear the dark blue veil off so that the baby could breathe the sweet air of life.

They say this midwife was also a voodoo woman. She exclaimed on the day Henri Roi was born, "*Hola, Sainne Vierge!* Do you know what this means? *C'est petite bwoi la* has the eye for *les mauvais esprits*—ghosts! *Pour les affaires autre mondial.* He and the sea will have no problem, 'cause he bless on the water. But on the land, he will die like any man."

So this was Henri's provenance. He could see ghosts, and he would not die upon the waters—a lucky thing if you are a fisherman. And he was, or so he did become, in the passage of time. Oh, the stories one could tell! Legends so tangled they bear strange fruit. Truth is, little is known about Henri Roi's early life. Except that he wasn't born in the lap of luxury, but in the palm of the poor, so to say. He learned early on that only the fittest of the fittest survive.

Henri's parents passed on before he was ten years of age. After that he became not a street kid or a beggar but a diver of coins. Tourists on the great cruise ships flung coins to Henri and others who swam deep to get them. Henri was one who never used "a glass," a face mask. He didn't need one. He dived. He chased coins like a fish. He filled his plastic scandal bag before anyone else.

Henri always ate well and provided for himself; however, as he was always alone, he became more and more selfish. He didn't share his winnings with anyone or help them gain theirs. People said he growled like a dog when he ate. So he grew up lonely, but he was famous nonetheless for his deep diving. The word was, "Henri never go bottom." Which did not mean that he'd never seen the bottom of the sea; indeed he had. No, it simply meant, he couldn't drown. Fishermen had seen him go off Twelve Saints' Rock, where the blue water is very deep. Down he went, eighty feet or more. For what reason did he dive so deep? He wanted to see the jewfish that lived there; no other reason.

Then came his greatest test, the one that truly sealed his fame as a swimmer of the somber sea. Henri, when he was fifteen and well turned out—he had a big barrel chest and a large square head and arms thick as gumbo-limbo—got a job as a cabin boy on a schooner called the *Hampstead*. This was a fifty-ton ship, which one day got caught in a squall one hundred miles off Bequia in the Windward Islands of the West Indies. Everyone on board knew the ship was sinking, and they ran like rats to save themselves.

Henri saw how fast the *Hampstead* was taking on water and beginning to roll, but he wanted to get to his cabin. There was a fine pair of fins in his locker. Henri ran belowdecks. However, before he got to his cabin, the *Hampstead* rolled and went straight to the bottom of the sea. As the vessel slid one hundred, two hundred, three hundred feet in a matter of minutes, Henri Roi struggled to get up on deck.

Through the fading corridors, some still dimly lit with guttering electric lights, Henri passed men who grabbed at his shirt, his pants, his flesh. They clawed at him. One man even tore at his hair. As he shot forward and out onto the sunken deck, the greenish light of the sea bottom met his open eyes, but no one clung to him anymore. He was alone at three hundred feet. Barefoot, he pushed free of the *Hampstead.*

Henri then followed the storm of silver bubbles. His lungs burned. He blacked out before he reached the turbulent surface. But he made it to the top. Henri came bursting up into the presence of two other men. The three held on as the squall continued. They were the only survivors of the *Hampstead.* One hundred and fifty-eight men had drowned.

It is a strange and unspeakable thing, a sinking ship. Many men going down on such a vessel say they see their lives flash before their eyes. But this was not the case with Henri Roi. He saw no departing life, no angel of death. He felt no soul scraping at his throat to escape out of his mouth. Nothing like that happened to him.

However, he did feel something new as he held on to the two other survivors. And it was something akin to love. Since the age of nine he'd lived alone, depending on no one but himself. Yet now, for some reason, Henri wanted to save someone, and it wasn't himself. It was as if having come from the bottom of the sea, the very bottom, he knew that he was unsinkable. But he saw the men's wild eyes and their fearful faces.

For the first time since he was born, Henri understood the perishability of human life. Human beings were afraid of dying, whereas for Henri the threat of death was much less than the burden of living. I must help them, I must save them, no matter what, he thought. I myself am nothing unless I save these men.

Some say he was touched by God. Others claim the devil saved him. Whatever magic spark ignited the selfish soul of Henri Roi, he was now changed.

"We gonna make it," he told the others. "I not gonna let you drown. I got the Great Maker in my heart and King Neptune in my bones; I can swim forever. This sea, this angry sea, is nothing to me."

The two men listened to Henri shout above the ocean's wrath. They clung to him. "Don't worry," Henri said, "I can save you. My legs churn. Rest, rest. I carry you."

They did as he told them to do.

And in the long night that followed, one of the men fell sound asleep. At length he lost his grip on Henri's shoulder. Henri felt the hand come loose. Desperately he tried to reach out for the dreamer, who was drifting away. But he couldn't let go of the other man, who was curled up like a baby. Henri watched in horror as the dreamer, the man who wouldn't wake, slipped off, white-faced, into the black night. Now there was only one other to care for, to hope for. Henri vowed that as long as he lived, this one would, too.

He swam all that night and into the morning. The sun rose blood hot. The sky cleared. The sea flattened somewhat, and Henri still swam while his friend hung on to his shirt and mumbled into his ear. They were each salt-mouthed, throats dry as a biscuit.

It rained. Henri raised up his head and caught some random raindrops. "We need some catchment," he said.

"All I have got is this," said the other, and he produced his teeth, his false teeth. The two of them laughed.

Henri said, "*Un moment*, that's not a bad idea." Then he took the dentures in his hand and held them open to the rain, and they caught precious drops. The two drank from the dentures. This was a great piece of luck because as it was, the sea was too rough to enable them to tilt back their heads and just drink in the falling raindrops. After the rain stopped, Henri resumed swimming. His companion held on to his shirttail and floated.

That day passed, and it was their third day afloat. Henri, ever the swimmer, was still strong. The other fellow, however, kept falling asleep. Henri had to slap him awake. "We two gonna die, you don't hustle your flipper a little." He was worried that the man would fall asleep and not wake up. The sharer of the shirttail nodded vaguely. He was dying; they both knew it.

Henri swam on while the sun baked the crown of his head and burned his shoulder blades crimson. When sundown came, Henri cried with relief. But his friend said nothing, for he was too weary to move his face or to hold on to Henri's shirttail. So Henri was obliged to cradle him in his arms once again.

All night he swam like that, pedaling with his legs, and into the fourth day.

At last Henri could carry the fellow no more. "Must

me got to haul you roun', man?" Bulb-eyed, his companion sank from sight. Henri dived down, brought him up. "You not gonna do that," Henri said. "You not gonna go bottom on me. I carry you so far, baby, I can carry you all the way to the moon, but you don't say nuthin' no more. Just talk in my ear like you used to."

The man said, "I can't talk over the singing."

"What singing?"

"The mermaids."

"There's no mermaids!" Henri shouted.

"Then what's that singing?"

"I hear nuthin' of it."

"Maybe it's angels," the dying man said.

Henri understood that his friend was raving mad. There was only the sea and the sky and the stillness. There was the brief wake he carved through the silent sea, but that was all. Henri was too tired to argue. His arms ached; he badly wanted to put his burden down. But he wouldn't do that on account of the promise he'd made to himself and to God Almighty. So he swam on.

Once at midday some flying fish struck him in the face. A dozen or more came winging low across the horizon. They skipped over the iron-colored ocean. When the flying fish caught the sunlight, they gleamed like white gold. Henri captured a few of them in his hand, but he had to let go of his friend to do so. He thought his friend would choke when he brought him up again, but he didn't make a sound.

"Eat, baby," he begged. "Eat so we will live to see another day." Henri ripped the wings off the little fish and ate them raw. His friend looked at him glassy-eyed, his head loose like a doll's. He wouldn't eat the fish, so Henri chewed them for him and pushed the paste of their salty flesh into the man's mouth. That way he got some nourishment down into him, not much but a little. Perhaps that little was enough to stay alive. As for Henri, the flying fish sustained him, strengthened him, gave him reason to swim on.

It was toward sunset that the miracle occurred.

The sea grew gray all at once, and the bottom came up to meet them. Henri and his half-dead companion found themselves on a tiny island. The strange barnacled land was thirty or forty feet long and about eight or ten feet wide. It was the smallest island in the world.

In fact, to Henri, it felt as if it was moving, but that was not possible. Islands do not float. Or do they? This one did. It cruised steadily through the sea at about two or three knots. Henri stretched out and slept. His friend did the same. And they lay, asleep, on the back of a whale.

All through the night the whale carried them, and they slept knowing nothing but the dreamless sleep of the near dead. Henri saw faces. He heard bells. He remembered the earth, how beautiful it was. He remembered laughter and the loveliness of it spilling out of his mouth and drenching the air like the tears of the Lord. In the darkness he remembered.

Henri woke up. His great gray island was sinking. It was going down into the depths. He scrambled to hold on. Then his lifesaving island, the whale, was gone. He floundered in the empty sea. Swimming, Henri thought of his friend. He splashed about, looking for him. In the wake of the whale Henri called out for him. He was struck by the fact that he didn't know the man's name. He'd never asked. Henri sobbed at his own frailty. His inhumanity. He cried out, "Baby, baby, baby."

Now he was alone. All alone in the secret sea.

It was then he understood a terrible thing. There *was* no other man; there never had been. He, Henri, was crazy. Was there ever a whale? Or was there just the lunatic Henri? This lonely boy swimming all by himself in the immense ocean? No, he decided, the whale was real. He could still feel its rubbery skin. But the men left him with no memory of solid flesh.

He was alive, the boy named Henri Roi. He said his name to make sure. Said it aloud, again and again. Then he began to shout. The name fell away on his tongue. Was there anyone to hear it? His voice curled off into the cosmos, into infinity. Henri understood that no one but God could hear his wailing.

For what seemed like a lifetime, he drifted. Neither awake nor asleep, he floated until at last he opened his eyes. He was lying on a long tawny beach. His body and head—all but his eyes—were completely wrapped in sargassum weed. You could not tell his top from his bottom, his head from his foot. Mummied in weed, he appeared neither dead nor alive, but a thing that was immovable. Like some charred island-grown tree that had been at sea for years and had at last rolled up on this Bequian beach as a burned-out, water-soaked log, which had traveled around the world, perhaps.

Henri had come full circle.

A woman who was painting a picture liked the way the log looked, and she included it in her seascape. When she put the finishing touches on her work, she noticed what might've been a foot protruding from the log. Nonsense, she thought, I am seeing things. When you stare at an object long enough, it always turns into something else.

The thing that resembled a foot twitched. The other end of the log made a croaking sound. That was how the woman knew the thing was alive. She ran down the beach to get her husband, and told him that she'd found a sea creature. "It looks like a poor dolphin all tangled up in some weed."

"Dolphins beach themselves on purpose," the husband said. "They come to land to die like whales. There's nothing we can do."

"But you must come and look," the woman said.

"I'm not sure I want to see a dying dolphin," the man said.

"Please," the woman begged.

"Does it smell?" the man asked.

"Terribly," the woman replied.

"This is my vacation, and I don't want to ruin it with a dead dolphin."

The woman gave in reluctantly. A half-dead dolphin, which could not be saved anyway, wasn't worth an argument on such a glorious sun-filled day at the beach.

Into that night Henri Roi remained alive, but barely. He lay on the unforgiving land, on the earth that was not as kind to him as the water was. He lay still amid shapes and sounds, none of which he could see or hear sharply. Spiritually Henri was beyond the physical senses. He existed somewhere in the dreamtime, the gulf between life and death.

A second miracle happened.

Two island boys running after a land crab tripped on something soft. They turned their flashlight on it. They knew at once it was a dead man. Yet the dead do not speak usually. This dead did; it talked some mumbly language of its own. They ran home to their shack and told their father, a fisherman. He was the one who got Henri to the hospital.

After Henri was extracted from the weed, the skin of his upper body—scorched and soaked and brined— peeled off like a layer of rotten newspaper. However, he lived. There were skin grafts, and he became whole again.

In time he returned to the sea as a fisherman, wanting nothing except the few fish that it took to keep him going.

Henri became a legend. And as often happens with a mythical being who is also a living man, he was surrounded with a kind of aura that made people wish to stay away from him. If it was true, as people said, that angels had saved him at sea, then he was not human. If, therefore, Henri Roi was immortal, few took comfort in his presence. They were awed by him, afraid of him, even jealous of him. But secretly they wished he would die, so that he might prove himself to be just like them, mortal after all.

One thing about the natives of Bequia made them like islanders everywhere. They said, "We are like crabs in a barrel. When one of us gets to the top and becomes something, the rest of us pull him back down again. That way no one gets out of the barrel, and we all remain the same." It was Henri Roi's unique freedom from the general rule that polarized his fellows and made them keep him at a distance.

One day, however, Henri was given a third miracle. This happened more than twenty years after his legendary swim. He was at sea in the Tobago Cays on his small skiff, fishing for tuna. Nearby there was another boat where a diver with a wet suit and tank was spearfishing for grouper. Henri saw that the man in the yacht performed his tasks with ease and precision. He went down, he came up—always with fish. Henri judged the man was a leisure-time fisherman; he fished with a spear for the sport of it.

And then the thing happened: The man with the speargun went down as before, but he came up differently. His glass was not on his face properly, and his tank was gone. Henri did only what instinct told him to do. He jumped in and saved the man from drowning. In fact, the stranger was barely alive when Henri got to him. Henri drew the water out of his lungs and breathed air into them.

The drowning man lived, and Henri got him to a

hospital. Then Henri went back to his own solitary life on the sea. He didn't know that the man he'd saved was later flown to Grenada, where he spent a month recovering from his bout with the bends.

Eventually, when Henri was back on Bequia, eating at a fishermen's café called Quick Drink, the diver he'd saved walked up to him and sat down at his table. Henri recognized the man's close-cropped white beard and sorrowful eyes. "I don't believe you and I have been properly introduced," the man said. "My name is Alexander Thompson; you can call me Alex. Do you remember me?"

Henri said, "Grouper man that go too deep. I pull you out of the sea, sometime year past." He returned to devouring his curried crab.

"May I buy you a beer?" Alex asked.

"Sure."

"What kind?"

"Any kind."

Alex could see that Henri wasn't much of a talker. "May I ask you a question?"

Henri, not looking up from his plate, nodded.

Alex asked, "If I said I'd give you anything your heart desired, what would you say?"

Henri shrugged. "For what?"

"For saving my life."

"That was nothing."

"I will be thanking you for the rest of my life. But I would like to do something for you as well. Perhaps something to change your own life for the better. It would be my way of showing you how much I treasure what you did for me."

"Mister," Henri said, looking up, "you don't got to thank me—*de rien* . . . nothing."

Alex laughed. "I know what *de rien* means; I come from Canada. All right, I'm done with being sentimental. But I still want to reward you somehow. I must. It's my nature."

Henri replied, "My nature's to eat when I hungry. Sleep when I tired. Pull people out of the sea when they drowning."

Alex laughed again. "Listen," he said, "I have plenty of money. And I'll tell you what—I'd like to share my wealth with you. I'm perfectly serious. You have only to accept my offer."

Henri pushed his empty plate away from him. He glanced into Alex's eyes, saw that he was on the level, and said, "Me? I don't doubt you are rich. I see your boat, the one you dive from. That is a rich man boat. Now, let me tell *you* something about me. You see, well, they say I am a man who don't go bottom."

Alex rubbed his chin. "You don't *what?*"

"I don't kill easily."

"Well, who does, besides a murderer?"

"I don't *dead* easily!"

Alex knew what Henri was saying. "Okay. It's clear now," he replied.

"So . . . " Henri belched into his fist. "I am such a man," he said, "who don't dead easy. So what do I care for silver or gold? I am richer, by far, than anyone I know. Them call me"—he gestured at the local people over by the bamboo bar—*"Henri l'immortelle."*

"Henri the Immortal," mumbled Alex. "I see your point," he said. "Let me restate my proposal to you, Henri. I live on a small island off the coast of Canada. The fishing there is excellent. I've always wanted to catch fish and sell them for a fair price. Here the waters are getting fished out. There aren't enough fish to feed these islands."

Henri's eyes clouded. "Would you put these poor fishermen out of work?"

Alex shook his head. "I'd hire them to work for us. Not as fishermen but as distributors of seafood throughout the islands. Loaves and fishes. You must have read about that in the Bible."

Henri smiled.

Alex went on excitedly. "I need a fishing partner."

Henri squinted at the light coming through his half-filled bottle of beer. "You think this thing could work?"

"*Bien sûr*, my friend. And while we're operating our business, we'll be putting money into this economy, giving people jobs, and best of all, we'll give the reef a little rest and let the fish propagate."

"Is it cold up there where you live?"

"I won't lie, it's chilly all right. But the truth is, we'd be there only part of the time. Most of the time we'd be here distributing our fish." Alex saw Henri softening to his proposal, so he added, "Besides, I'd have a partner, a friend, someone to talk to."

"I don't talk much."

"I'll do the talking then."

"What happen if we fall to a quarrel?"

"I love a good fight," Alex replied.

Henri asked, "Are you in good with the land?"

"Do you mean, am I as easy on *land* as you are on *water?*"

Henri looked up from under his heavy brows and nodded again.

"Well, I wouldn't call myself immortal," Alex said, "but my feet are pretty well planted."

Henri grinned. "A man with grace on the sea and a man with good luck on the land. It's not bad combination."

"Not bad," Alex replied. They shook hands and became partners in a plan that is still as solid as the day they shook hands on it. At any rate, they're still in the business of putting food into the mouths of the poor. And these two unlikely partners have not fallen to a quarrel yet.

Crossing the Everglades

When Walter Dimock decided to cross the Everglades in a canoe in 1929, he had a number of reasons for doing so. The time had come, he thought, to turn his life around. And to put it bluntly, he was broke; he owed a lot of money because of bad real estate investments. Florida was the great land of boom or bust, of fortunes made and lost, and Dimock had lost. His Green Acres Paradise Land Parcels, Inc., had gone broke with a lot of money owing and none coming in.

So for Dimock it was time to close accounts, as they

say. The back door was wide open to the Everglades. All he had to do was relocate from Fort Myers to Miami, the sparkling new city freshly claimed from the mangrove mire of the swamps, and he'd be safe to start over.

Miami was gleaming with glamour. A man could get capital there without any curious questions.

Dimock's plan was to disappear into the Ten Thousand Islands and go from there into the Everglades. Tom Osceola, a Seminole friend and trail guide, offered to help Dimock.

In the end they didn't take the standard stuff—no tents, canned food, medical equipment, or anything to ease the burden of a long trip through the trackless channels of the quaking grass. Instead they brought only what Tom required them to bring: two knives, a couple of spoons, cups, forks, plates, and, of course, a canoe.

"I think we might need more than that," Dimock said. The trip was going to be nerve-wracking enough without the simplest of amenities. Actually, Dimock didn't like camping. He liked the Glades even less. Most of all, he despised being poor. He was not made for scrabbling or hard-luck losses. Maybe his choices hadn't been the best. Still, he wasn't ready to declare himself the victim and let his creditors pick him apart like a bunch of vultures. One thing about the Glades: A man could lose himself in there. Not be found until he wanted to be. Meanwhile, his trail—if a trail on water is one at all—would disappear. If Dimock had to eat turtle in a chickee hut with Tom Osceola, so be it. Better that than the prison up in the panhandle.

Tom gave in to Dimock's desire for a few luxuries. "All right." He grinned. "For you, I'll bring along a coffeepot and a frying pan." Then he added, "Let's go whole hog—bacon, cornmeal, and enough ground coffee to last for a couple of weeks. What are you going to bring?"

Dimock answered, "My Stevens double-barrel shotgun."

Tom Osceola pushed the black forelock out of his way. His dark eyes twinkled. He had a round head and a stocky body. He looked as if he were always at ease. Even standing, he seemed to be sleeping. But Dimock knew different. Tom had a way of seeing without looking. He was good at it.

"What else should we carry?" Dimock asked. "How about a wool blanket, rubber sheet, mosquito bar, and how about a change of underwear?"

Tom shrugged. "I don't wear any."

"Well, I suppose that's best, since we're trying to travel light."

They shoved off at Billie Creek in southeast Fort Myers at dusk. Shortly thereafter, they entered the ocean-going flow of the Caloosahatchee River, and their journey was begun. It was the dry month of March. The weather was clear. The canoe was loaded, and so was the shotgun. There was nothing ahead of them except Chokoloskee Bay, the Ten Thousand Islands, Turners River, and the strung-out bays of Sunday, Huston, and Chevalier. It seemed easy enough, but Dimock had his doubts.

There were revenue officers who patrolled the bays by powerboat and gators and saltwater crocs that never stopped looking for an easy meal. Panthers, too—those tallowy, gold ghosts—screamed in the night and were known to stalk human beings. Then there were the hefty mosquitoes that reduced beef cattle to bones. And the black-tipped sharks and the bull sharks that hunted the shallows of every salty river mouth, bumping canoers into the water and devouring them a chunk at a time.

First night out, they camped in the yard of an abandoned sisal plantation on Pine Island.

"The owner of this place," Tom said, "went off to Cape Sable, I heard. There was a warrant for his arrest, but no one was willing to serve it to him."

"Why not?" Dimock wanted to know.

"Well," Tom said as he brought their things out of the canoe, "the fugitive, this fellow named Mr. Wilson, was handy with a gun. Seems he shaved off one half of a warrant officer's mustache before the deputies even got a good look at him."

Dimock shifted from one foot to the other. "Maybe they should've left him alone. What was his crime, anyway? Trying to put food on the table?"

Tom grinned. "He made bootleg whiskey and buried it in casks on all the little mangrove islands. I should say, he *had* it buried. Mr. Wilson, they say, didn't like this country much. He liked that big house yonder. Stayed in it all the time, playing solitaire with his gun on his lap."

"You think he'll be coming back here anytime soon?" Dimock asked.

"Might. Depends."

"On what?"

"Whether he wants to."

Dimock thought about that as he looked at the big house made out of pink conch shells. It gave off an eerie glow in the dense magenta dusk under the peeling, rusty-looking bark of the gumbo-limbo trees and the heavy-leaved Cuban laurels. The island, the pink house, and the haunted trees looked unfriendly and weird.

As they made camp in front of the house, Dimock thought of Wanted Wilson. Tom had said everyone thereabouts knew of him. He had been a local hero, reportedly giving away his money to the poor—a Robin Hood type. But he had gotten caught. And gotten away. Sooner or later everybody gets snooped on, Dimock decided. That reminded Dimock of his own rotten-luck land deals. Every man, he said to himself, is a good man in a bad time. It was hard as hell to survive anywhere these days, but it was nearly impossible in the backwaters of southwest Florida.

While Dimock gathered buttonwood sticks for the fire, Tom went into Wanted Wilson's former garden. It was overgrown, but there were some sweet potatoes, and he was going to roast them on guava coals. The night was cracking with frogs and so thick with mosquitoes that the only way to get rid of them was to sit half into the fire.

Tom cut some of Wilson's sugarcane for dessert. The two men stirred their coffee with it while they listened to the trilling of the screech owls. Somewhere, not too far off, a bull gator bellowed. They went to sleep under their mosquito bars, their separate tents of gauzelike netting. Dimock lay for a long time, listening to Tom snore and to the soft beating of moths' wings against the gauze. The night droned on as the shrill nocturnal insects drilled at the layers of darkness.

What a place to live, Dimock thought. He tried to imagine Wanted Wilson in that huge blob of a house made of pink conch. Built like a fortress, it gave off a pinky glow even after nightfall. Dimock smiled as he visualized the warrant officer getting his mustache surgically removed by Wilson's bullet. Finally Dimock's eyelids grew heavy. Poor Wilson. Poor man in this awful wilderness.

And then Dimock dreamed.

He saw Wanted Wilson, barefoot in the pepper-colored sand. He was wearing a crisp white Havana suit. Wilson was smiling as if he knew who Dimock was. With a start Dimock woke.

Leaves crackled. The wind brought the sweet confection of night-blooming jasmine and the haunted face of Wanted Wilson close to Dimock's mosquito bar.

"Who are you?" Wilson said.

A horned owl pumped off five hollow hoots.

"Am I dreaming?" Dimock asked aloud.

The image of pale Wilson melted away.

There was a noise, *crrunch!*

Dimock sat up.

A key deer the size of a small dog bounded off into the predawn darkness. Dimock sighed, lay back down. He was damp with sweat, and a little wheeze was scratching at his throat. It took him a long, long time to fall asleep again.

When he woke, the morning sun lay aslant in long pencil-like bars that pierced the upper layers of the olive leaves.

Tom grunted, "Good morning." He offered Dimock some avocado pears on a piece of corn bread. The heavy, salty air was braced with the smell of boiled coffee and bacon.

"You hear anything last night?" Dimock asked.

Tom's black eyes gleamed with humor. "One of Wilson's pet deers. Forgot to tell you he had 'em. Got 'em off Big Pine Key."

Dimock imagined how pretty the Wilson property must have looked, once upon a time: the well-tended gardens, the pruned trees, the tame deer walking daintily in the shadows. Wilson had an eye for beauty, Dimock thought. Not just for whiskey money.

Most of that day they paddled hard, punishing themselves in the heat on the trip to Alligator Bay. It was a long, hot haul through the waterlands. Orchids clung to the trees. Some, Dimock observed, looked as somber as a Quaker lady; others were costumed to rival the queen of Sheba. These were weird, fluid flowers befitting the place that bore them.

On one of the keys of Alligator Bay they found a plume bird rookery. The egrets had been killed for their feathers. The adult birds were either gone or sacked; the dead left to rot in the sun, leaving the young ones to starve. It was a horrible scene. Dimock felt grateful that he had Tom with him because Tom knew where he was going. Without a guide, the wetlands were a death-trap. There were desperate people, as well as fierce animals, that lived among the mangrove islands. Dimock didn't know which he feared more: the wild people or the wilder critters.

Every time Tom went away, which was fairly often, Dimock feared that he wouldn't come back. He always did, but his absences were worrisome to Dimock.

Mostly Tom went off looking for game, but sometimes he'd leave just to be rid of Dimock for a while.

As the iodine-tainted night settled, the canoers found a crooked creek where the plume hunters had felled cypress to block the passage of the game wardens. More miles of navigation through little lakes, rivers, and keys, and it was finally time to put up for the night . . . but where? They either had to sleep in the canoe, cramped up, or somehow find a dry piece of land, which wasn't presenting itself. The mosquitoes came in choruses, singing mournfully, ebbing and flowing.

Tom caught sight of some banana plants poking out of a little hammock. He waded in first. "Stay in the canoe," he said. "I'll be right back."

The black water was up to Tom's armpits. Soon Dimock couldn't see him; it was too dark. But he could hear him, sloshing. Then, except for the grunting frogs, there was intermittent silence.

Tom pushing branches back; then quiet.

Tom *plook*ing through the mud; then stillness.

"What are you doing?" Dimock called out.

No answer. Time passed. It seemed, after Dimock had waited and heard nothing, to be at least an hour of silence. He sat, swatting mosquitoes, wondering where Tom was. Had the Glades reeled him in and wrapped him up in a cocoon?

Dimock's heart thudded. Something's happened to Tom, he thought. "Tom!" Dimock hollered.

The frogs, in mid-chorus, caught their breath, after which the croaks came on, one after another, piling and tumbling into a great gob of gratery voices.

At last Tom said, "Over here." A match flared. A cone

of light illumined Tom's face. He was parting the fans of some arrowroot leaves.

"Come in with the canoe," he said. "Look out, though. There's hardly any headroom when you get in here."

Tom had found the only piece of solid earth anywhere around. As Dimock got into the water to guide the canoe under the pressingly low limbs of the cay, he felt something squirm with startling speed under his right foot. It felt like a thick, knotted water moccasin. Dark and triangular-headed with a mouth white as cotton, the moccasin was quick to strike from the ground, the water, or even a low-lying mangrove limb. Rattlers coiled and struck—but only on land. Moccasins hammered at you from anywhere. They were nasty-tempered, fiercely territorial serpents.

Dimock walked with a new caution in every step.

Tom, however, was slopping around, trying to catch a bullfrog. "Here's one the gators won't get." He chuckled as they dragged their canoe onto the tiny hardwood hammock. There was just enough room for the two of them on the little cay.

Tom skinned, cleaned, and roasted the bullfrog over a

campfire. Along with the frog, there were some short, fat, starchy wild bananas and a few hard little half-ripe guavas. There was space for one man to sleep in the canoe. The other had to lie curled on the ground. They drew straws. Tom got dirt; Dimock, the canoe.

The mosquito bar spread over the top of him, Dimock had only to worry about the mosquitoes that had already found a haven inside the canoe. He slapped at them, but it didn't seem to reduce their ranks.

Then it started to rain. After not getting wet, Dimock realized it wasn't rain falling lightly on his head. It was palmetto bug wings; something up above was eating one bug after another. The thing, whatever it was, was sitting on a limb just over his head.

The unknown palmetto bug predator prompted Dimock to have a nightmare. It was about a beast that the Seminoles said lived in the Glades. A cross between a skunk and an ape, it was a hulking manlike creature that scratched its back like a bear against the tall yellow pines.

"Its hair," Tom had told him, "is over a foot long."

"You don't *believe* this, do you?" Dimock had asked.

"I don't *dis*believe it," Tom had answered.

In Dimock's nightmare the skunk-ape's eyes were blue-green like little wax myrtle berries. The teeth brown as the tea-colored tannin creeks of the Glades. Across the face, a white skunk stripe.

For two days after that night on the hammock, Dimock and Tom Osceola made good time. They slipped through forks and bights and bunchgrass prairies. More than once while paddling, Dimock thought of Wilson. Narrow-shouldered and sharp-eyed, Wilson rested his cheek on a rifle stock. His lips were smeared with a funny little come-get-me grin.

One afternoon Tom slipped away into a hardwood hammock, with no explanation of where he was going, or why. He was gone a long time. Dimock found himself growing more and more worried. Where had Tom gone? What if he didn't come back?

Dimock fretted for an hour or more before Tom appeared smiling. "Want some palmetto honey?"

Once they found a deserted Miccosukee cay surrounded by wild lime and lemon trees and miles of white and yellow water lilies. Tom made lime juice with water and cane sugar, and they were quenching their thirst when the two men heard the dry buzz of a diamondback rattler.

Dimock jerked up as if by an electric jolt. Tom remained squatting on his hams.

The snake was curled under a lime tree, its tail moving feverishly.

Dimock grabbed his shotgun.

Tom said, "That's just the keeper of the swamp."

But before Tom could stop him, Dimock took aim. The gun boomed. A heron *grawk*ed. The whole hammock rocked. The blue smoke quavered, hesitated, hung in the air.

The big snake writhed, twisting in spasms. Both men were motionless. After a while the serpent finally stopped coiling and uncoiling.

Then Tom laid it out, dead, on the charcoal-colored sand. The diamond markings, patterned to look like leaves, were speckled and painted with sunlight and blood.

"You killed the grandfather that guards this place," Tom said.

"It was kill or be killed," Dimock answered. But even as he said it, his words seemed empty. Killing the great snake sickened him as much as fear had turned his stomach when he first saw it.

Tom respectfully hung the long, half-gutted, heavily muscled rattlesnake on a swamp maple branch. He sprinkled pinches of cornmeal from a little leather bag he kept in his pocket. "This is the way we do it, our way," he said. "The place was cursed by your gun, but now I've given it a blessing."

After this, they left the cay and paddled south toward Miami.

"You're really mad at me." Dimock said after a long silence.

Tom nodded. "Your luck's going to change for the worse."

"Couldn't get much *worse* than it is," Dimock said. "Sounds like you put a curse on me, Tom."

Somewhere off in the mangrove maze across the vast brown blanket of saw grass darkly dappled with little islands, there was a panther howling. The cat's screams seemed to trigger the sudden downpour of rain. One moment it was clear; the next it was not. The sky and the land were one great wash of blue-black. Lightning forks flickered through like a snake's tongue, lighting up the jungly thickets. There was nothing to do in the deluge except push on through the crowded bonnets of water lilies, the soaking, croaking evening full of dimpled water and darting danger.

Time passed, and they continued to paddle in silence. Dimock, soaked to the bone, went off on a fantasy about Wilson. He couldn't have said why the man was so much in his thoughts or why he had become a mixture of everything that opposed Dimock in the Glades. One man had become synonymous with the critters, the mud, the choking lilies, the poisonous snakes, and the urgent feeling that he, Dimock, was completely cast away. His greatest fear was that Tom Osceola would disappear for good. The Glades pressed down on Dimock's soul. Every wagging beard of grizzly gray moss gave him the spooks.

After the rain, the setting sun filtered through the bulk of blackish clouds, and the Glades dripped and creaked and oozed. Cicadas whined. Frogs rotored and roared. Leaden-coated herons went by with a *woof-woof-woof* of wings, and then a party of rusty-colored ibis flew down the lanes of misty, grassy rivers.

Dimock wasn't cheered by any of this. He thought, The creatures know where they're going; I do not. He imagined Miami, bright white, rising majestically out of the labyrinth of the Glades. He prized the image of a city large enough to be lost in. It was possible, probable even, that being lost in a place like Miami was like being found. Streets, avenues, boulevards—these were things that Dimock knew and understood. You could, he believed, wrest whatever you wanted from them. But what could you take from the Glades that it wouldn't demand back?

Thinking such gloomy thoughts, Dimock felt the descending darkness fall about his shoulders. They came to a Miccosukee fish camp that had been recently abandoned. It was an island of an acre and a half, fringed with pawpaws, wild grapes, and cocoa plums. Piles of sun-whitened turtle and snail shells lay about, along with the larger bones of deer and the finer fish-bones of mullet, gar, and bream. All this Dimock saw as Tom built up a large fire. Under a huge, dead mastic tree there was a chickee hut with a thatched roof.

"Let me borrow your shotgun," Tom said.

"What for?"

"I want to shoot us some supper."

"What kind?"

Tom answered, "I saw a possum back in there."

"Roast possum would be good," Dimock said.

He gave Tom the gun and some shells. Tom crunched off into the brush.

Dimock looked beyond the margin of the flames. All around, the hot sea of saw grass smelled of decay, rotting humus, and ruinous roots that arched like spiders over their prey. In the deeper water the red, glowing lantern eyes of alligators patrolled the island.

What's to keep them from coming up here? Dimock thought. I haven't got my gun anymore. The possibility of Tom's not returning cracked through his mind again. Dimock threw more dead buttonwood on the fire. The wood was damp, and it exuded a grim, heavy smoke that lay about his ankles and came up to his nostrils smelling of acrid bark. There was nothing to do but feed the fire and wait.

Hours passed.

Dimock was beside himself with unnamable fears. Always there was weird little Wilson, bare-chested with red suspenders. His ruthless eyes mocked Dimock's cowardice.

Suddenly Tom appeared, holding a possum by the tail. "Didn't have to use your gun after all," he said.

Dimock was greatly relieved to have his gun back. "Where are the shells?" he asked.

"Oh," Tom answered, "they slipped out of my pocket. I don't have them anymore."

"You—*what?*"

Unconcerned, Tom started humming a little chant as he dressed out the possum and prepared to cook it on the fire coals. "The Great Maker has seen us through another day," Tom said. The possum flesh began to sizzle and steam over the low flames.

"How did you get it without the gun?"

"I used my knife. Possums don't move when they're hanging upside down on a limb."

"I don't see how killing this animal is *good* but my killing that snake was *bad*." Dimock spoke crossly.

"You wouldn't understand if I told you," Tom remarked.

"Try me."

But Tom only said, "You killed a great snake, a grandfather. With the Maker's blessing, this little possum will feed us, and I asked if I could take his life, so that we might live ourselves, and I was told yes, go ahead and live, two-legged man; take this four-legged and go about your way."

"I sought the same blessing when I killed the rattlesnake," Dimock said. Stubbornly he insisted he was not wrong in killing something that might have tried to kill him or Tom.

Tom's black hair lay straight and long to just about his shoulders. His bangs gleamed in the light. "That old snake wouldn't have done us any harm, nor would its flesh have tasted any good if you'd tried eating it. You killed him out of fear. Why don't you just admit it?"

Dimock felt hot. Tom was mocking him, like Wilson. "You're *always* right, aren't you, Tom?"

Tom Osceola did not say anything. He cooked the possum, ate some, left the rest for Dimock. Then he unrolled his mosquito bar and blanket and went to sleep without another word.

The night echoed with omens. Dimock picked at the possum. The roasted meat tasted sweet in spite of the bad words he'd had with Tom. He ate as much as he wanted; then he built up the fire. Alligators cruised silently all around this end of the island. Dimock could see the orange embers of their eyes. He was too afraid to sleep. He'd given Tom his shotgun shells, and Tom had lost them. Then he'd had to throw the rest away because they'd gotten soaked in that downpour. The outcome was that there was no more ammunition.

All through the night Dimock sat up by the fire, feeding it and watching the lazy predatory circles of the alligators. The dying rattler, Tom's curse, the skunk-ape, Wilson, especially Wilson—all these came into his mind, flickering like the firelight. Once, toward morning, a huge garfish jumped and made a loud splash. The alligators surrounded the fish and tore it apart. Dimock shivered as he watched the spectacle. He clutched his gun. It would make a good battering ram, he thought.

In the dawnlight Tom emerged from his good sleep well satisfied. He was not friendly to Dimock, but he seemed inwardly happy. They left without breakfast, according to Tom's whim. After a few hours of quiet paddling, they came upon a Miccosukee man who said his village was close by. Tom knew where it was, and they went there.

There were more chickee huts with palm thatch roofs. The earth was well tamped by bare feet. The hard, swept eating area was neat and clean. Dimock noticed that the women wore full long skirts, but the men wore merely long shirts that hung to the knees above their bare brown legs. They were friendly enough. They offered Dimock some sofkee mush in a gourd bowl. Dimock was starved. He fell upon it when it was given to him.

After he ate, Dimock walked around. Tom seemed to have disappeared, as usual. Each one of the open-air, thatch roof chickee houses had a clock in it, but none of them worked. All the dead clocks were stopped at different hours. For some reason, seeing this made Dimock feel crazy. It was as if for him, the time of the outside world had died. Was this the curse brought on by killing the rattlesnake?

Tom came out of the mangroves in someone else's

canoe. He was poling this one, not paddling it. He brought it to the sand and got out, barefoot, and walked up to Dimock.

"I need to get paid," he said. "There's a man I owe some money to, and he wants it now."

Dimock said, "You'll get paid when you deliver me to Miami."

"We're about five hours from there now," Tom told him.

"I won't pay you a penny until you've put me down on a cement street."

"Is that because you haven't got it?" Tom asked. His eyes narrowed, and his lower lip was pushed out.

"I have it, and you'll get it when I say you will."

Tom glanced into Dimock's angry eyes. He, too, looked angry. But only for a moment. "Have it your way," he said, and then he got back into the strange log canoe and poled away from the shoreline.

After Tom left, the other Indians, one by one, went their separate ways by water and by land. The island seemed quite large, and some of them disappeared into the cypresses and the silence. The gray beards of Spanish moss barely moved in the hot, swampy air.

By late afternoon Tom had still not returned. A few other Indians had come back, but they were busy fixing fishing nets, and they didn't talk at all. None of them answered Dimock when he asked if they'd seen Tom.

Well, Dimock's worst fear was realized: Tom Osceola had left him for good. He could feel it; the man was gone, no question. He went off without his money, Dimock muttered to himself.

Then Dimock got into the canoe that belonged to Tom, and he shoved off in what he knew was the direction of Miami. He was sure of that because Tom had pointed to the southeast, and where else would Miami be? That was where it was, and he paddled there as hard as he could, trying to make up for lost time.

While he dipped his paddle and drove the canoe forward, Dimock focused his thoughts on the distance that had been covered. They'd been out a week and had paddled nearly one hundred fifty miles through mosquitoes and sand flies and bull gators and diamondbacks, and they were—at least Dimock was—out of harm's way now that Miami was so close, so close he could almost smell it. The swamp was dwindling, too.

The waterway was widening, and the great swamp was shrinking, and the distance was faintly glowing along the horizon line.

This watercourse is none other than the Miami River, Dimock told himself. He wondered if Wilson had come this same way in his escape from the law. "One more night in this stink hole, and I'll be free and clear," he mumbled.

Then, all of a sudden, he remembered Tom's curse. For a second he saw the huge snake thrust and twist, exposing the yellow, smooth belly scales in its death throes. He forced the picture out of his mind. He hadn't far to go.

That night it sprinkled. Luckily Dimock came to a hunter's cabin built on stilts alongside the river. It was empty. He tied Tom's canoe to the dock and went up the tall, crooked stairs to the cabin.

Inside, the place smelled sour and closed up. There were turtle shells and other ancient refuse on the floor, but at least it was a floor—he hadn't seen one made of wood in a week. He bedded down. However, the dripping rain and the steady leaks from the sagging roof caused him to haul Tom's canoe inside and position it upside down between two cast-off chairs. This was a fair roof, and even though his feet got a little wet, his head was dry.

The stairs leading up to this stilted house were many, and all night Dimock imagined he heard feet on them. It was only the rain, he told himself, but he couldn't shake the feeling that lurking out in the shadows was the skunk-ape. A wet, dark thought. But he couldn't shake it.

The screech owls began to whinny in the crosshatched Australian pines. Dimock started to sweat out his worst fears. The breeze sucked the ragged cotton curtains out the open windows of the stilt house. Dimock sneezed. The place stank of mouse droppings. The broken front door creaked on a rusty hinge. Tree frogs cheeped; leopard frogs droned; bullfrogs groaned. There was a scuffing sound on the bottom stair.

Dimock drew a deep breath.

One stair.

Then another.

Click.

Click.

As if an afflicted foot were dragging. Dimock's heart jumped and banged against his ribs. He wished Tom hadn't lost the shells. He felt in his pants pocket. Something cool to the touch was in there. The familiar shape told him it was a cigarette lighter.

Now, in his exhausted mind, Dimock assembled the familiar face with the black and white striped fur and the low, ledgy brow. He saw the sharp incisors between the parted lips.

He stiffened, listened.

Three stairs . . . now girding up for the fourth.

Click,

  click.

How many stairs to go? Nine, ten? The night fear boiled out of him like sweat from a turpentine pine. His mouth was dry as a fishbone. His heart thudded: *plum-plump, plum-plump.* Was there a weapon anywhere in the cabin? In the thin starlight of the broken window, Dimock saw a discarded boot.

The slow ascent continued. First one foot, then another. The heavy body bore down on the stair planks.

One foot, *chickawx*. Then the other, *chickawx*. Dimock stumbled to his feet. Fumbling for the boot, he reached out, got it. His other hand went deep into his pocket and brought out his lighter. Great, a lighter and a boot against the skunk-ape. Dimock shivered. His empty shotgun was halfway across the room.

A toe click, followed by a heel scrape.

Crix, craxt.

Then, mid-stair, the thing crouched to strike. Dimock could feel its readiness. Adrenaline rocketed through him. Ready to scream, bash boot, throw lighter. Yet there was a fragment of reason left in him. A small voice said, "Get ahold of yourself, man." He would've if he could've. The problem was, it was too late for that. Heartpoundingpumping was so loud it had to be audible outside his own head. The skunk-ape had to be listening, sensing his fright.

The wind came up; the door cracked wider. Dimock blinked. There was nothing there. Are you crazy? he said to himself. He stood at the open doorway, and there was only the empty stairway.

"Where are you?" he said aloud.

A screech owl answered with a tremolo whimper.

For a long time Dimock stood in the starlight. *Ploop!* *Ploop!* Raindrops were falling off the rusted tin roof. Disgusted with himself, Dimock went back to his mosquito bar and lay down. Well, if there was no skunk-ape, then what was he afraid of? Tom Osceola's curse? That was nothing. He'd make amends, somehow. Tom's money? He'd send it to him, plus something extra for the canoe. He'd never kill a snake again, that was for sure.

His random thoughts returned once more to the Glades and his obsession with Wilson, who was, in his mind, less a man than a creature of the river of grass. Like the skunk-ape, like all the other animals, real and imagined, Wilson was a mystery. When you entered the dark veils of the labyrinth, the Glades, you became part of the trembling waters, part of their haunted watery identity. And you lost something of your old self, while something of the skunk-ape crept into your soul.

Dimock sighed. The screech owl seemed to answer him with a faint, fractured sobbing. Well, if crossing the Glades had taught Dimock anything about life and about himself, it was how to look fear in the face and not run away from it. Oh, he'd been running all right. But as hard as he'd paddled, the Glades had pulled him back. Dimock felt their irresistible force now, even as he lay at the edge of the quivering saw grass swamp.

For a week straight and across one hundred fifty miles of meandering streams, Dimock had traveled and faced his nemesis: fear. He was still facing it in this falling-down stilt house. Dimock wondered if Tom, when he saw him again, would see his newfound strength. But maybe, like the Glades, it lay beneath the surface and was nothing you could put your finger on.

The Modern Mariner
and the Pilot of the *Pinta*

*I*n 1892 Logan Welsh was working in Gloucester, Massachusetts, as the harbormaster. He fitted the part, too, with his square beard the color of ripened wheat and his short-visored captain's cap. However, there was something about him that seemed restless and out of place. It was almost as if he had a double somewhere who was living the life he really wanted to live himself.

Now, one day Logan made an enemy of a captain he'd once worked for as a cabin boy. Harry Hapchance was the captain's name, and a rougher sort of one-eyed seaman wasn't to be found in the city of Gloucester, or anywhere, for that matter.

"I could'na see a bloomin' thing but the fog!" cried the offended captain when Logan accused him of bumping and sinking a fisherman's skiff in the harbor that morning.

"Can you see this?" Logan asked, handing him his summons.

"Youngster," said Captain Hapchance, who remembered Logan's rebellious ways aboard his schooner when the harbormaster was still a cabin boy, "I'll post your little goat's beard on my mizzenmast if you don't tear up that summons!"

Logan replied firmly, "You'll pay your harbor fine and render up a boat for the fishermen that you've put out of work, sir." Logan spoke as if Truth were a solid pillar of salt that belonged, solely and irrefutably, to him.

Captain Hapchance rolled his good eye, while his other, a frosted ball of glass, fixed upon nothing in particular. "I've a notion that if you'd been behind the helm, you'd have struck the skiff yourself, Mr. Welsh. For as I say, it wasn't my doing at all, 'twas the fisherman's fault, as any of my men will tell you."

Logan Welsh, however, didn't budge. In the end the summons stuck, and Hapchance paid the fine with a grumble and an oath. At the Farthing Tavern, he swore to another skipper, "I'll rid us of this ironclad young harbormaster, who never sees but one side of the issue, his own. I've a plan, and you'll see it working soon enough."

The other skipper raised his mug of grog and asked Hapchance what he had in mind.

"I've a passion for hatching plots," the captain crowed, his glass eye riveted to a ceiling beam. "But this one'll be simply laid. I'll offer our self-righteous harbormaster something he cannot refuse, a ticket to the Seven Seas!"

The other skipper said, "But the boy loves his work here. He'll never leave Gloucester!"

"The young whelp hasn't really met the sea as a full-fledged captain yet. With the right opportunity, he'll be off and away."

The manner in which this sleight of hand was accomplished was less devious than might be imagined. First, Hapchance did his duty: He bought a skiff and duly gave it over to the fisherman whose relic he'd bumped in the harbor that ill-fated morning.

After this, he hired a team of mules to haul a worthless wreck of a sloop from the foamy cobbles of New Bedford. Hapchance made a present of this hulk to Logan Welsh. On the surface the gesture was a peace offering to Logan, but what a stinking gift! The sorry-looking, seaweed-laden sloop was an offense to the eye and nose of all who passed it.

At first, of course, Logan didn't want it; who would? But when Logan tried to refuse it, the crafty old sea dog gave him a wry, twisted smile. "My gift to you, sir, for my rude behavior, thereby to diminish your wrath and have you forgive my roughish ways. May the old hulk delight your fancy and tease you into making her into a craft worthy of your talents."

Logan looked upon Hapchance in surprise. "Talents? What talents?"

"Oh, I know a proper sea captain when I see one. From the day I first laid eye on you as a mere stripling lad, I saw you were cut for the cloth of captain. Indeed, I did. You're no harbormaster, Welsh, even though you hide under the guise of one. You're a captain, born and bred, which is why you ride so high and mighty upon your fancy rules of conduct. Just like a captain, I say!"

"Is this a bribe or a joke?" Logan asked.

"Neither," snapped Hapchance. "It's the work of Fate. What will be, will be."

So now Logan Welsh had a boat, such as she was . . . or would be . . . or could be. There she lay in such disreputable shape. The skeleton of a dismasted sloop, lying on her side in front of his porch. What would he do with her? It gnawed at him. A day did not pass that he didn't cast his harbormaster's eye to that hideous wreck that lay ruinous and insulting in his yard.

What happened was that Logan, little by little, started to clean up the mess. He carted off rotten timber, and in some weeks' time, what had seemed a detriment began to appear as a diamond in the rough. The classic lines of the old sloop began to show. People noticed, and complimented Logan. Maybe there was a ship there after all. At the same time, Logan Welsh underwent some changes himself—from straitlaced harbormaster to weekend boatbuilder. In no time he developed a passion for the work. Ruggedly he pitted himself against the sloop, which he had decided to name *Fancy Free*. For months, then, whenever he had a spare moment, he was out there in his yard working. He felled an oak tree and carved a solid oak keel. He cut white oak stanchions for the ribs and yellow and white pine planks for the deck. Thus the thirty-six-foot sloop went from a derelict to a beauty of the brine, all in just thirteen months. The *Fancy Free* measured nine tons net, twelve tons gross. Total cost to Logan: $553.62. So now he had a freshly painted, perfectly appointed sailing boat.

What to do?

Logan followed some ancient instinct, which his very soul required. He quit his job as harbormaster and launched the *Fancy Free* as a fishing boat. In this endeavor Logan was a failure. For one thing, he had no heart in it; he had no cunning for baiting hooks. For another, the cod weren't exactly plentiful that season.

But the thing that surprised him was his skill as a mariner. He was as deft as the best of them, and he read the stars and the deeps as if they had been charted in his own head.

Logan started a journal. From his first day until his last he kept daily records of his voyages. "I am going to find out whether I am made of the same stuff as my father and my brothers. I want to see if I am as accountable as a sea captain as I was as a harbormaster. The sea is a great teacher: It teaches those who are courageously wise and those who are wisely courageous. I hope I will be something of both."

When he set off in 1895, Logan had few provisions and little enough comfort. But in this, he was satisfied. He planned to improvise as he went along, figuring that this, too, would be part of his great quest of survival. In the little berth that he called home, there was a smashed-face clock that he'd bought for a dollar and a two-burner table lamp that served as a cooking stove. He also stored away a tub of lard, a barrel of potatoes, six casks of water, and enough raw sugar and flour to last for a long voyage. These, plus a cabin spider (with wife and children, as he thought of them), were all, besides Logan himself, that the *Fancy Free* ferried as he made his way across the Atlantic to Gibraltar.

He quickly fell into the habit of giving commands

and answering them. One night he lashed the rudder, so he could stay down in the cabin. But he found himself calling up to the deck: "How goes it there, my man?" Then, in a different sort of tone, he said, "All's well, Cap, all's well."

In this way Logan whiled away the hours. Next day he was at it again. When the sun was at the meridian, he shouted, "Eight bells!" and then answered in another tone, "Eight? Already?" Day after day he kept up this playful talk. The other thing he took pleasure in was singing. He couldn't hold a tune. But it was fun to sing, anyway.

Logan's first sense of fearful isolation came upon him when he sailed away from Nova Scotia and entered the Atlantic. On this, his farewell to land, he watched the lights blink away for the last time. When the last little beacons of gold were gone, he found himself in a fog so thick, he imagined he might walk upon it. It was as if his loneliness had been made visible and turned into phantoms of fog.

Still, he held tightly to his figurative compass, which was a clear mind and the common sense of his New

Bedford forefathers. Yet even when he slept, he dreamed he was alone. The night sky enforced his solitude supreme, yet it was also a spectacular show of heavenly spheres. The sea, too, sparkled with light shows.

One night he glimpsed a thing that confused him. It was a calm sea. On the surface of the water there appeared a dancing fire, to which his eye was deeply attracted. A glowing path. Logan stared hard, trying to use his mind to discern what it was he was seeing. The last quarter of the moon wasn't bright enough to be lighting up the sea with burning ghosts. The shapes loomed and shrank.

Then he remembered something a captain had once told him about: phosphorescent plankton. So it was nothing more than a bunch of microscopic imps flaring at the bow of his sloop. But then suddenly the little fire points came apart. Out of the agitated water a round, shining head appeared.

Was this a creature of the sea? Or some unknown being from the sky, thus fallen from heaven? Logan's heart started to leap. Then he realized he was looking at a porpoise. The cheerful mammal was floating in the ocean's fire. Gradually Logan settled down, no longer afraid, and watched the porpoise's antics.

One afternoon, as Logan was entering a harbor outside Fayal in the Azores, he saw a pirate ship anchored close by. He examined the crew with his telescope. Rowdy sailors, wearing scimitars and carrying pistols and billets, were coming to greet him.

"What do we do now, Captain?" Logan called out to himself in the playful voice of a deckhand. He replied in his best captain's voice, "Let's see how many costumes we can show the beggars. Give them as many clever entrances and exits as Mr. Will Shakespeare!"

"Capital idea!" barked the mate. "But what exactly do you mean, sir?"

"Watch, and I'll show you," said the crafty captain.

Quickly Logan made up a dummy sailor. He buttoned his heavy blue coat around a piece of bowsprit, which he'd sawed off in Buenas Aires because it was damaged. Then he stuffed his pillow inside his coat and added a pair of trousers, plumped up with salvage trysail. The dummy had a coconut head and a stocking cap. In short order, his ruse offered the image of a sailor lying on the bowsprit. By tying a piece of twine to the arm of the coat, Logan could secretly pull the coat sleeve aloft so that the arm appeared to be pointing at something. It looked real enough to fool Logan himself.

When this was accomplished, Logan dropped into the cabin and threw on another set of clothes. By then the pirates had lowered their dinghy and were coming toward him on a fair wind from across the bay. Out of the forescuttle Logan came trundling, flashing his machete in the red afternoon sun. At the same time, with his toes, he jerked the line attached to the seaman's coat, and up went the dummied arm, as if saluting an order.

Then, going into the cabin again, Logan redressed and came up in his Sunday harbormaster's getup. After showing himself this way for a few minutes, he sloughed off his good clothes and popped out of the forescuttle, naked as a native with a loincloth made from a scarf. Because his skin was varnished bronze from the sun, Logan looked like a Bornean wild man with tousled hair. Altogether his inventiveness created five different crew members, a hardy lot, and no easy pickings for pirates!

When the brigands saw the number of men aboard the *Fancy Free*, they went back to bolster their forces. Meanwhile, the wind freshened and Logan set full sail and left port.

This proved a great lesson to Logan. Madness, he decided, is not to be feared when it is used for survival. It is in fact the very substance of the survival instinct. He reasoned that his own ancestors had conquered beasts in just this way. What is cleverness but a softer intention of madness?

In Morocco, moored in a harbor the color of cinnamon and cream, Logan was attacked again, this time at night. Hearing the thump of an oar against the curve of his bow, he knew the *Fancy Free* was about to be boarded. What to do? He envisioned burnoosed midnight raiders with drawn daggers. There was no time to do anything but lock his companion hatch, which he was doing when he stepped on a tack. As he plucked it out, the pain shot all the way up his leg. It hurt, but it gave him a crazy idea.

Hastily he got out the can of tacks that he'd bartered for in Gibraltar. Before buckling down the hatch, he cast the tacks in a circle on the deck. Then, locked up and listening, he heard the dull thud of bare feet come from above. There was quiet, then scuffling. Followed by painful howls. A horrible hopping. This gave Logan no end of pleasure, especially since the rascals immediately repaired to their dinghy and, with a swarm of oaths, pushed off. Listening to the plumping of their oars, Logan laughed. Once again, he'd proved that spontaneous thinking could save the day, or the night, as it were.

In the palm-fringed Canary Islands, Logan went ashore and harvested coconuts, not only for their water but for their meat. Some of this he sun-dried on deck. The rest he boiled over the flame of his double-globed oil lamp. Once the coconut was rendered and cooled, he scraped the congealed substance into his frying pan.

After this, Logan grated the coconut meat and mixed it with flour and raw sugar. When the coconut oil was hot, he cooked golden brown doughnuts. These were so delicious he made up a song about them:

Doughnuts, doughnuts, made from coconuts.

The shape is round, the recipe's sound,

But the flavor will make you go nuts!

Logan ate a bunch of them and saved the rest, thinking he might be able to trade them for a few things he needed. In fact, the following day at a local bazaar, he traded his doughnuts for some rare spices that came in little banana leaf packets sewn with palm twine. The packets were full of yellow curry, rust saffron, red-brown paprika, as well as earth-colored cumin, salt, pepper, and sugar.

That night a school of young squid, chased on the starlit waters by a shark or barracuda, jumped out of the sea and landed with a thump on the deck of the *Fancy Free*. One jumped so hard and fast that it struck Logan full in the face and knocked him down. Lying on his side, he stared into the clicking parrot's beak of the angry-eyed creature.

After recovering from his amazement that such an intricate creature could exist, Logan picked up the violet-hued animal, filleted it, laid it in oil, and fried it over his oil lamp stove. The squid was deliciously sweet and tasted nothing like it looked.

And so it was, and so it went. In his meditative, meandering way, Logan sailed around the world, meeting things he had never dreamed about but which existed and were as commonplace as he was. Wherever he went, he survived by his innocence and his wit.

In Rio de Janeiro, for instance, he put on an ingenious little show and charged sixpence to see it. What Logan did was catch a shark and ride it all around the deck. He sat on the shark's back and held on to its dorsal fin. The animal was very much alive. Thrashing and bucking from bow to stern, the shark drew a paid crowd of spectators. This little enterprise brought Logan enough money to buy some canvas sails, of which he was badly in need.

There was another time, when heading for Cape Horn, that Logan stopped at a barren volcanic island, where a man traded ten chickens, a rooster, and a goat for an equal number of Solingen steel fishhooks. Now the chickens were generally good company, but after being their friends, he couldn't think of eating them, even though he dreamed of fried chicken every night. So they roosted in his rigging and defecated on his head when he was at the helm. For all his patience and tolerance, Logan didn't get a single egg out of those fowl.

The goat was considerably worse. He got into

everything and made a complete nuisance of himself. He liked to crunch cans in his teeth, and he ate the stuffing in Logan's only mattress. As if that weren't enough, the pesky goat chewed up Logan's favorite straw hat and his chart of the West Indies. The map he felt he could do without, but not the hat; it was the last straw, so to speak.

When he reached Timor, Logan unloaded his menagerie and took new bearings from a Dutch mariner that he met. This man rounded up his stock and gave him three casks of water, some rigging, a fishing net, and a much-needed pair of scissors. Logan sailed on to the Marquesas and then to Fiji, Samoa, and Australia. The wind was steady, and he lashed the rudder and spent fewer than three hours a day at the helm.

One day, when he came up on deck, the wind was so strong it blew a small yellow songbird into his hair. The bird leaned with the pull of the wind, its tiny claws caught in his wiry sun white hair. Then it lost its footing, and with a parting trill, it sailed off into the headwinds, skimming this way and that. To Logan, the bird was like himself. He'd get caught for a moment in the blue hair of the sea; then the wind would pick up, and he'd be off again, following the stars, the islands, the migratory birds, and the great schools of passing fish. All these knew where they were going, and Logan learned to trust them and follow their wheeling rounds across the seas.

Logan's time was well spent, he thought, talking to the husband spider, which he had named Most Perfect Boston Person. The spider was his friend and confidant. One day, on the coast of Mauritius, Logan took on some needed water, and while passing time filling casks at a small, clear stream, he chanced to see an African spider. This one was larger than the Boston variety, and Logan made the mistake of capturing it and bringing it back to the *Fancy Free* to meet MPBP.

In his innocence, Logan imagined this would be another companion to his friend, and what solace it would bring. Unfortunately it wrought havoc. MPBP, that trim Bostonian guarding his family, made mincemeat of the African spider, which was three times his size. Size counts for little, Logan reasoned after the battle was over. And it seemed to him that cleverness won the day in both human and spider worlds.

When Logan had been at sea for almost three years, he had an experience that shook his faith in his religion of reason. This thing that happened to him turned his life upside down. He had always prided himself in knowing the difference between illusion and reality. He could playact and spin fables with himself and with MPBP, but he never allowed himself the luxury of thinking that talking to a spider or an imaginary crew member was the real thing. Then something happened that caused Logan to reflect that the rational world he lived in was not as real as the world of the spirit, the one that he played in with his spider.

One day on the island of Pico in the Azores, he was offered some white cheese by a member of the American consulate. The last few weeks Logan had eaten mostly hard, dry bread and fish. The sight of the snowy cheese was almost maddening to him. He ate three curds, polishing it off with some Madeira wine and a half dozen plums. The combination made his ears burn. By nightfall, crouched in his cabin, he was still nibbling cheese crumbs that had fallen into his vest pocket.

A few hours later Logan was sick. It was a night he

could ill afford to be belowdeck, as a heavy sky to the southwest brought a severe storm his way. Reeling from cheese and wine and plums, Logan fell prey to cramps and delirium. He was too sick to stay at the helm or even to secure his sails. From time to time he woke with the sweat shining on his face, his eyes bulging and the whites yellow.

He was poisoned by bad cheese. In fact, he felt as if he were dying.

Awakening at one point, Logan found himself in a pounding sea. He looked out the companionway. There was a strange, tall man looming lustily at the helm. He had a head of oily black curls, tied at the ends with funny little silver ribbons, and he wore a stocking cap of red velvet, which flopped to his shoulder, tight-fitted leggings, and a fancy waistcoat. On his feet were black boots with Spanish buckles.

Logan shut his eyes. He had seen such men pictured in storybooks, but never in real life. Was the whole thing an apparition? He clutched his stomach and moaned. It was certainly possible his illness had conjured up the vision. But what if the stranger were real?

Logan forgot the storm that was battering the *Fancy Free* and held his stomach in pain.

"Have you come to cut my throat?" he asked at last. "If so, do it now. I'm sick to death, and I've no mind to stop you."

The black-whiskered man laughed, and his hair gleamed in the slanting rain. "I'll not harm you," he said in a booming voice. "I'm here to save you."

"There's little to save, I'm afraid."

"Are you quite mad?" the other asked.

"I've never been anything but sane."

"Well"—the stranger grinned as he wrestled with the wheel and fought the gale—"does a sane man stuff himself with cheese and plums and then go sailing off into a storm?"

Groaning, Logan shook his head. "How do you know what I ate? You weren't there! Nor do I think you're here with me now. It's all in my imagination."

The big man roared above the wind, "You think I'm not real? You think me a ghost?" He seemed incensed and amused at the same time. Then he said, "Let me introduce myself: I am Martín Alonso Pinzón, pilot of the *Pinta*. I've been looking after you for many hours, my friend. You've been quite a chore, with your errant ways."

"The *Pinta*?" Logan blinked and wiped the salt from his eyes.

"Come, come. You must know of it. The ship of Captain Columbus."

"Christopher Columbus?"

He looked at Logan with pity. "Is there any other?"

"Columbus lived hundreds of years ago."

Logan felt his head splitting and his stomach reeling. He could barely get up in the pitching sloop. "I'm dreaming," he mumbled to himself. He felt as if he were burning up.

"Look," said Martín as he fought the wheel, "it is mad to argue in a storm. Do you not see that ship over yonder?"

Logan squinted into the stinging beads of hard-driven rain. He looked out the companion, and in lightning-forked darkness, he saw a three-masted ship. Then, his headache and stomachache overcame him, and Logan sank back onto his mattress and fell unconscious.

He woke once more in the midst of the storm's worst lashing. Feeling the bolt of the bow and the moan of the mast, he wiped the sweat from his face and cried out, "My sails will be torn to ribbons."

"Not so," answered the helmsman. "But we have to catch up with the *Pinta*, so I need all the sail I've got."

"All's lost," Logan muttered into his sweat-soaked pillow.

Martín said from the creaking helm, "You did wrong to mix white cheese and plums, Captain Welsh."

"How do you know my name?"

But above the wind Martín asked him, "How do you think you've come so far? Didn't you ever wonder if it was a little more than a blessed beginner's fortune to travel so smooth across the seas?"

Logan sighed and clutched his belly. He had no answers and no more questions; he fell into a deep sleep.

In the morning he was better. He got up on deck and, finding no one there but himself, was greeted by a calm sea. He checked his chronometer and sextant. There were little islands dotting the horizon, and he measured them against his map. By Logan's reckoning, he was ninety miles from where he'd been the day before. On true course. This all had happened at night and on a maddened sea. It wasn't humanly possible. Still, it had happened.

A ghost had ferried him safely through a hurricane and gotten him to where he wanted to go.

From that day on Logan was a different man. He listened anew to the small unreasons of his heart. He seemed to believe that all things were possible and that nothing in God's realm was out of the ordinary. He began saying prayers morning, noon, and night. And he waited in hopeful anticipation of dreams that would take him to other worlds. Always he hoped for the return of the night visitor, Martín Alonso Pinzón, his savior. But though he prayed for his friend's return, Martín Alonso Pinzón did not reappear. Logan now acccepted the knowledge that angels guide the actions of humans, and this gave him a feeling of confidence and strength he'd never had before.

By 1898 Logan Welsh had returned home to North America. When he laid eyes on the North Star—he hadn't seen it in three years—he wept. He fought against a gale from the southwest until he rounded

Montauk Point at the end of Long Island. There, when he set foot on land, he heard rumors of war. America was fighting with Spain, and there were mines in the sea meadows of Newport Harbor.

Storms, bombs, and quakes of all kinds were old news to Logan Welsh, but it was when he returned to Gloucester that he had his second great lesson in unreason. Coming into the foggy harbor, he accidentally struck a fishing skiff and put a hole in it. While the little boat was bubbling, the harbormaster rowed out to meet Logan. And as it happened, it was none other than his old nemesis, Captain Hapchance.

"I see you've got my old hat on now," Logan said as he surveyed the damage he'd wrought.

Hapchance replied with a wink, "As do you, my friend."

"Does it suit you then?" Logan queried.

"It's a trifle boring after being at sea. How goes it with you, aside from coming in without due caution?"

"I came in on the tide after three years of wandering the seas. I'm as guilty as you were when I saw you last, so I must pay up, Captain. But I should also tell you that I haven't anything to show for my rambling but a hold full of shells and feathers."

Captain Hapchance was delighted with this admission of guilt and penury. "I see quite a new light in your eye, Captain Welsh. Who, or what, is it that put it there?"

Logan whistled through his teeth. He breathed the familiar air of his old home port with both pleasure and sadness. "I'm not the same man I was, Captain. Yet neither are you, I'm sure. It's odd we should end up like this, in reverse positions, so to say. But from what I've learned at sea, up is down and down is up."

"Your fine," said Captain Hapchance with a grin, "is to fix this poor man's boat before it goes down. Haul it up or sink it, it's all your responsibility. But as I know you're an honorable salt, the deed will be done before the morrow."

It was, too, for in addition to his skills as a helmsman, a sailor, an actor, a journal keeper, a philosopher, and a dreamer, Logan Welsh was an improviser and a craftsman of cunning skill. He fixed the boat up nicely and paid a visit that evening to the Farthing Tavern, where he sat on a stool beside the harbormaster, who bought him a drink.

"Tell me, man, what you have learned," Hapchance said. "I see a whole new person in that darkened skin of yours."

They touched grog glasses. Logan said, "I ought to thank you, friend, for setting me asail. I never could've known . . . that such things exist in this world of ours."

Hapchance grinned from ear to ear. "Such things as?"

Logan lowered his voice and said mysteriously, "Things greater than I can say, Captain. Why, from what I have seen and heard, the world is no larger than the head of a pin. Yet it is all a mystery to me now. A great and wondrous mystery, for which I am both thankful and humble."

Captain Hapchance was surprised to hear such talk from the same man who'd left Gloucester knowing so much more than anyone else.

Shortly thereafter the two men parted as friends. Logan grew restless in Gloucester, however, and was soon off around the world again.

In his sixtieth year Logan went up the Orinoco River in Venezuela. He was not seen again. The *Fancy Free* disappeared with her captain. Naturally, there were those who said that Logan Welsh had been apprehended by pirates and some who insisted he had been struck at night by a freighter that sank him without a trace.

Of course others who knew him, Captain Hapchance among them, told a different tale. "Logan lived in two worlds," Hapchance told the *Gloucester Gazette*, "this one of ours and the one of the spirit. It was the spirit world that Logan loved best. He told me that spirit sailing is the finest there is, no matter the weather."

To this day no one knows for certain what happened to Logan Welsh. Yet he set the world's first record for around-the-world sailing alone in a sloop. More important to him, he proved that a man could do anything he set his mind to. There are those, too, who say that Logan and the *Fancy Free* turn up from time to time when the hurricanes are blowing and some captain needs an extra set of hands on the wheel.

Endnotes

"THE TURTLE ISLAND OF PETER SERRANO" was suggested by "The Adventures of Peter Serrano" in *Great Shipwrecks and Castaways: Authentic Accounts of Adventures at Sea*, edited by Charles Neider (New York: Harper & Brothers, 1951). The original narrative contains a lot of interesting detail but very little core information about the shipwrecked man's feelings. It is known that he lived on the island first for three years alone and then for another four years with a companion. During this time Peter grew a protective covering of body hair and lived off sea turtles, using their shells as a kind of armor and their meat for food. After his rescue, Peter did in fact travel around Europe as a sideshow attraction. I emphasized in my story Peter's faith and the power of his personal vision. My tale may have a certain spiritual quality that is not found in the original narrative. In any case it is an interesting footnote that Peter's island off the coast of Peru still bears his name on nautical charts.

"THE BEASTS OF PHILIP ASHTON" is a story that combines many authentic personal narratives, two of which were found in *Great Shipwrecks and Castaways: Authentic Accounts of Adventures at Sea*, edited by Charles Neider (New York: Harper & Brothers, 1951). The two stories are "Philip Ashton's Own Account" and "The Just Vengeance of Heaven." However, there was not enough information in either story to create a suspenseful tale of a castaway who loses his mind. So I turned to two novels by Daniel Defoe: *The History and Remarkable Life of the Truly Honourable Colonel Jack*, first published in 1722, and *The Life, Adventures and Pyracies of the Famous*

Endnotes

Captain Singleton, first serialized 1720–1721.

The true story of Philip Ashton is pretty bare of detail. He was captured by pirates in 1722, then marooned. He lived for sixteen months in solitude on a desolate island, where he often feared to go into the water because of "shovel-nosed sharks" and alligators. There were wild boars on the island, and he expressed fear of them. He did meet a traveler who visited him in a canoe; this mild stranger came and went the way I describe it.

Ashton did not go crazy, as far as we know from his own account. In "The Just Vengeance of Heaven" there are specific references to madness of the narrator, Captain Mawson, who in 1725 found himself on the island of Ascension. Mawson believed his being marooned was a punishment from God and his suffering the result of crimes he'd committed in his life. The Mawson account gave me "the beasts" and the ill-sorted thoughts of a starving and mentally depraved person. I invented the specific odd encounters, hallucinations, and extreme paranoia of a man who is seduced by his loss of self.

The Triangle Islands also appear in Ashton's account, but he was not rescued by Caribs, as I have made out in my story. Many mariners *were* saved by Caribs, who have, in my opinion, an unjust reputation for cannibalism. The real Philip Ashton was rescued by an American merchant ship, while Captain Mawson died from starvation. Mawson's skeleton was found next to his journal, which had been written in his own blood. I put my story in the middle ground between these two endings.

"THE WIDOW CAREY'S CHICKENS" was inspired by J. S. Sleeper's historical narrative *Ocean Adventures* (Boston: Locke & Bubier, 1858). I changed Sleeper's account by adding characters and dialogue and by expanding upon the mystical powers of the widow Carey. Sleeper's narrative is an Isles of Scilly legend. In the original story Mrs. Carey is a beautiful woman who has been utterly desolated by tragedy. With little help from the natives of Bryher, she lives in an ancient temple that the islanders say was built by the Druids long ago. She attracts "stormy petrels." Sleeper suggests that the Druid temple, the tragic woman, and the birds are related in some mystical way. But he does not explain the mystic relationship.

In my version of the story I introduced other characters that would bring out the healing quality of the widow Carey. I thought she deserved more characterization than Sleeper gave her. He saw her primarily as a tragic figure. I saw her as one who might have been able to work miracles.

"THE MAN WHO WOULD NOT GO BOTTOM" was suggested by a myth in *Folklore and the Sea* by Horace Beck (Middletown, Conn.: Marine Historical Association and Wesleyan University Press, 1973). In the original version Henri Roi is named Henry King. I respectfully returned his name to its French origin. In the legend Henri performs the grand feats that I attribute to him in my tale. However, he doesn't meet a whale, nor does he become a business partner with anyone. He merely moves to Canada and isn't heard from again.

The whale comes from a true story I heard some twenty-five years ago. A family survived an airplane wreck at sea and were rescued by a humpback whale, which swam with them until they were spotted by a jet plane. A cousin of one of the participants told me their tale. The detail of the dentures came from an event that happened near our home on a barrier island in Florida. Three fishermen, capsized in the Gulf of Mexico, were saved by capturing rainwater in one of the men's dentures. The details of swimming for a long time in salt water are from my own long-distance swims.

"CROSSING THE EVERGLADES" was inspired by a story by A. W. Dimock, "Crossing the Everglades in a Power Boat," which appeared in *Tales of Old Florida*, edited by Frank Oppel and Tony Meisel (Secaucus, N.J.: Castle Books, 1987). Dimock's adventure took place in 1907. He was led by a Seminole guide named Tommy Osceola, and the trip followed the geography cited in my version. The two men actually traveled 146 miles in six and one half days. The dangers they met were ants, alligators, and a large rattlesnake. However, none of the fears and phobias that accompany my Dimock character are mentioned in the original story. There was also no antagonism or ambiguity in the relationship between the two men.

The bootlegger, Wanted Wilson, came from two sources. Such a man, mentioned in Dimock's story, was identified only as Wilson. From Dimock's report he shot off a warrant officer's mustache—half of it, anyway—with his gun. The other source was the Chokoloskee storyteller Totch Brown. Mr. Brown, whom I met and listened to shortly before his death in 1997, knew a great deal about the infamous Everglades criminal Mr. Watson. I based my Wilson on Brown's Watson.

The addition of the skunk-ape theme came from many stories that are still current in the part of Florida where I live.

"THE MODERN MARINER AND THE PILOT OF THE PINTA" came from the life of the nineteenth- and twentieth-century sailor Joshua Slocum. I used two books for my research: *Alone at Sea: The Adventures of Joshua Slocum* by Ann Spencer (Buffalo, N.Y.: Firefly Books, 1999) and *Sailing Alone Around the World* by Captain Joshua Slocum (New York: Century Company, 1900).

Most of the details in my story follow this amazing mariner's real exploits. He rebuilt a boat in which he sailed around the world. In fact, he was the first man to sail around the world alone. The cost of rebuilding his sloop, *The Spray*, was thirteen months' labor and $553.62 in materials. He had adventures with pirates and with the ghost from the *Pinta*. His observations and his pet spider were taken from fact. He weighed anchor in 1895 from Yarmouth, Massachusetts, and returned three years later to Montauk Point, Long Island. He still holds the record for the most miles traveled and the greatest number of places visited by one man in a sailing vessel.

My story diverges from his in a number of ways. I used the name Logan Welsh for my character because I wanted some additional freedom in which to fictionalize Slocum's beginning and ending as a mariner. I gave Welsh a solid reason for leaving his home port, and I made his disappearance at the end of his life something more spiritual than Slocum's supposed robbery and murder on the Orinoco River. It is believed that Slocum ended up unbalanced from being too much alone at sea. As for his death, no one really knows what happened to him because his vessel and remains were never found. Personally, I liked the idea of bringing his life and death full circle. It seemed fitting that my character Logan Welsh should have two spiritual benefactors, Captain Hapchance and Martín Alonso Pinzón. One starts him off on his journey, the other saves him and perhaps ferries him into the hereafter.

GERALD HAUSMAN is the author of more than fifty books for children and adults, many of them dealing with the theme of survival. As a licensed scuba diver and lifeguard he has had many marine adventures of his own, from when he was a Sea Scout in the 1960s into the present. From 1985 to 1993 Mr. Hausman ran the Blue Harbour School of Creative Writing on the island of Jamaica. There he taught a course in long-distance swimming, taking groups of boys and girls open-sea swimming to the offshore island of Cabarita on the north coast. The distance covered was two and a half miles each way, and he and his students swam without assistance in an incoming and outgoing current between the mainland and the island. This experience helped in the writing of several of the stories in this book. Today Gerald and his coauthor wife, Loretta, live on a Gulf island in Florida with two Great Danes, a Siamese cat, a European shorthair, and a blue-fronted Amazonian parrot. When not in the water, Gerald is busy writing or telling stories at schools, universities, and conferences.